DREAM OF DRAGONS

(AGE OF THE SORCERERS – BOOK EIGHT)

MORGAN RICE

Morgan Rice

Morgan Rice is the #1 bestselling and USA Today bestselling author of the epic fantasy series THE SORCERER'S RING, comprising seventeen books; of the #1 bestselling series THE VAMPIRE JOURNALS, comprising twelve books; of the #1 bestselling series THE SURVIVAL TRILOGY, a post-apocalyptic thriller comprising three books; of the epic fantasy series KINGS AND SORCERERS, comprising six books; of the epic fantasy series OF CROWNS AND GLORY, comprising eight books; of the epic fantasy series A THRONE FOR SISTERS, comprising eight books; of the new science fiction series THE INVASION CHRONICLES, comprising four books; of the fantasy series OLIVER BLUE AND THE SCHOOL FOR SEERS, comprising four books; of the fantasy series THE WAY OF STEEL, comprising four books; of the fantasy series AGE OF THE SORCERERS, comprising eight books; and if the new fantasy series SHADOWSEER, comprising three books (and counting). Morgan's books are available in audio and print editions, and translations are available in over 25 languages.

Morgan loves to hear from you, so please feel free to visit www.morganricebooks.com to join the email list, receive a free book, receive free giveaways, download the free app, get the latest exclusive news, connect on Facebook and Twitter, and stay in touch!

Want free books?

Subscribe to Morgan Rice's email list and receive 4 free books, 3 free maps, 1 free app, 1 free game, 1 free graphic novel, and exclusive giveaways! To subscribe, visit: www.morganricebooks.com

Select Acclaim for Morgan Rice

"If you thought that there was no reason left for living after the end of THE SORCERER'S RING series, you were wrong. In RISE OF THE DRAGONS Morgan Rice has come up with what promises to be another brilliant series, immersing us in a fantasy of trolls and dragons, of valor, honor, courage, magic and faith in your destiny. Morgan has managed again to produce a strong set of characters that make us cheer for them on every page....Recommended for the permanent library of all readers that love a well-written fantasy."
--*Books and Movie Reviews*
Roberto Mattos

"An action packed fantasy sure to please fans of Morgan Rice's previous novels, along with fans of works such as THE INHERITANCE CYCLE by Christopher Paolini.... Fans of Young Adult Fiction will devour this latest work by Rice and beg for more."
--*The Wanderer, A Literary Journal* (regarding *Rise of the Dragons*)

"A spirited fantasy that weaves elements of mystery and intrigue into its story line. *A Quest of Heroes* is all about the making of courage and about realizing a life purpose that leads to growth, maturity, and excellence....For those seeking meaty fantasy adventures, the protagonists, devices, and action provide a vigorous set of encounters that focus well on Thor's evolution from a dreamy child to a young adult facing impossible odds for survival....Only the beginning of what promises to be an epic young adult series."
--*Midwest Book Review* (D. Donovan, eBook Reviewer)

"THE SORCERER'S RING has all the ingredients for an instant success: plots, counterplots, mystery, valiant knights, and blossoming relationships replete with broken hearts, deception and betrayal. It will keep you entertained for hours, and will satisfy all ages. Recommended for the permanent library of all fantasy readers."
--*Books and Movie Reviews*, Roberto Mattos

BOOKS BY MORGAN RICE

SHADOWSEER
SHADOWDEER: LONDON (Book #1)
SHADOWSEER: PARIS (Book #2)
SHADOWSEER: MUNICH (Book #3)
SHADOWSEER: ROME (Book #4)
SHADOWSEER: ATHENS (Book #5)

AGE OF THE SORCERERS
REALM OF DRAGONS (Book #1)
THRONE OF DRAGONS (Book #2)
BORN OF DRAGONS (Book #3)
RING OF DRAGONS (Book #4)
CROWN OF DRAGONS (Book #5)
DUSK OF DRAGONS (Book #6)
SHIELD OF DRAGONS (Book #7)
DREAM OF DRAGONS (Book #8)

OLIVER BLUE AND THE SCHOOL FOR SEERS
THE MAGIC FACTORY (Book #1)
THE ORB OF KANDRA (Book #2)
THE OBSIDIANS (Book #3)
THE SCEPTOR OF FIRE (Book #4)

THE INVASION CHRONICLES
TRANSMISSION (Book #1)
ARRIVAL (Book #2)
ASCENT (Book #3)
RETURN (Book #4)

THE WAY OF STEEL
ONLY THE WORTHY (Book #1)
ONLY THE VALIANT (Book #2)
ONLY THE DESTINED (Book #3)
ONLY THE BOLD (Book #4)

A THRONE FOR SISTERS
A THRONE FOR SISTERS (Book #1)

A COURT FOR THIEVES (Book #2)
A SONG FOR ORPHANS (Book #3)
A DIRGE FOR PRINCES (Book #4)
A JEWEL FOR ROYALS (BOOK #5)
A KISS FOR QUEENS (BOOK #6)
A CROWN FOR ASSASSINS (Book #7)
A CLASP FOR HEIRS (Book #8)

OF CROWNS AND GLORY
SLAVE, WARRIOR, QUEEN (Book #1)
ROGUE, PRISONER, PRINCESS (Book #2)
KNIGHT, HEIR, PRINCE (Book #3)
REBEL, PAWN, KING (Book #4)
SOLDIER, BROTHER, SORCERER (Book #5)
HERO, TRAITOR, DAUGHTER (Book #6)
RULER, RIVAL, EXILE (Book #7)
VICTOR, VANQUISHED, SON (Book #8)

KINGS AND SORCERERS
RISE OF THE DRAGONS (Book #1)
RISE OF THE VALIANT (Book #2)
THE WEIGHT OF HONOR (Book #3)
A FORGE OF VALOR (Book #4)
A REALM OF SHADOWS (Book #5)
NIGHT OF THE BOLD (Book #6)

THE SORCERER'S RING
A QUEST OF HEROES (Book #1)
A MARCH OF KINGS (Book #2)
A FATE OF DRAGONS (Book #3)
A CRY OF HONOR (Book #4)
A VOW OF GLORY (Book #5)
A CHARGE OF VALOR (Book #6)
A RITE OF SWORDS (Book #7)
A GRANT OF ARMS (Book #8)
A SKY OF SPELLS (Book #9)
A SEA OF SHIELDS (Book #10)
A REIGN OF STEEL (Book #11)
A LAND OF FIRE (Book #12)

CHAPTER ONE

Nerra clung to Shadr's back while the great black dragon flew north and east, devouring the landscape in powerful wingbeats. With each one, Nerra had to fight against the urge to simply let go and tumble from the dragon's back, seeing if her scaled, blue Perfected form would survive the smashing impact against the ground below. The robes she wore flapped in the wind, and Nerra had to set her reptilian face against its sting.

You will not be permitted to fall, Shadr said, the words echoing in her mind. *Have no fear, my Chosen, I would catch you.*

It wasn't fear Nerra was feeling, though. Instead, wave after wave of grief filled her, building up inside her with no way to break free. She wanted to cry, but it seemed that her Perfected form had no tears in it, that such a thing was a strange remnant of the human life she had set aside.

You are stronger now, Shadr said. *You have no need for the weaknesses of the human things.*

Shadr's presence seemed to fill her, the dragon's mind and power so great that Nerra felt as if she might burst with it. The dragon's presence was like a dam, and all Nerra's grief was pent up behind it, unable to come through.

I will protect you, Shadr said, *from all that might harm you.*

"You killed my brother!" Nerra called out, over the rush of the wind. "Were you protecting me from him?"

Shadr's presence meant that she couldn't feel all of the pain of that, but even so, Nerra ached with it. She could still remember the moment when Shadr's claw had come down, piercing Greave, when she had lifted him and used her flames on his flesh as if he were no more than a sheep or an ox to be devoured.

He was no more than that, Shadr said. *He was a human-thing, an animal without the connection to magic of dragons, without the transformation of the Perfected, or even the Lesser. His loss means nothing, save that you are free from one more chain binding you to that old life. You are mine, not theirs!*

1

Once again, Nerra felt that thread of fierce, possessive jealousy coming from the dragon queen, so that anything that wasn't hers had to be destroyed. Nerra was hers, and so she could not have a family, could not mention the dragon she had found as a hatchling…

Do not think of that one!

… could not even have her thoughts to herself. Shadr's wings powered her on over the countryside, and all Nerra could do was cling to her back, her grief pushed down inside her, waiting for whatever her queen would decide she had to do next. Nerra pushed against that presence, but it was too great.

Astare came into view on the horizon. The city that had held the great library of the House of Scholars was changed now beyond recognition. The outer city that had once stood there to hold those visiting its more ancient heart was largely gone, either burned or simply torn down by the dragons who had descended on it. The inner city remained, constructed from strange obsidian buildings built according to some geometry that had made sense only to the scholars. They formed squares, spires, and domes that had once been part of a greater pattern; now they stood largely empty.

Dragons were using those buildings for perches, some curled up like cats on the sunniest parts so that they could bask, others rearing with wings spread. Here and there, gouts of flame or frost or lightning shot into the sky, in displays of power and magical control. A kaleidoscope of different-colored dragons covered the rooftops, or flew above them in elegant, swooping displays. A green dragon flew low beneath Shadr as they approached, and a golden one flew past with a horse in its jaws, reminding Nerra uncomfortably of those Shadr had brought down in the ambush of her brother.

Around the dragons, the Perfected moved and fussed, bringing them what they required, following their orders, the humanoid lizard-folk's scales shimmering as they went. The greater mass of the Lesser surrounded the city, ebbing and flowing like a tide, their animal screams and roars a cacophony without cease, controlled only by those of the Perfected who moved among them to command them. Some still sat on barges out beyond Astare, a whole navy of them waiting to pour out across the kingdom.

Nerra knew that there were former friends of hers down there, people from the Isle of Tears, those who had suffered from the Dragon

2

Sickness and been transformed. How many were Perfected like her now? How many were Lesser?

It does not matter, Shadr said. *They are what they were always meant to be. In any case, the business of the transformed and the human-things does not matter now. We must speak with our kind.*

Shadr swooped in a circuit around the inner city, banking left and then curving slowly around to her right. Below, the dragons there spread their wings and lowered their heads in submission, in respect for their queen. They made a low, rumbling sound that reminded Nerra of a thousand voices all humming the same note, and that note rose up in a roar of welcome for the most powerful among them.

Looking down, Nerra could see the obvious arrangement of how the dragons were perched. The most powerful got the highest and largest perches, while the less powerful got lower, smaller spots. Among them, Nerra could see those who sported wounds from small battles for position, challenges among dragons usually continuing until one or the other of them conceded defeat. Shadr had been the only dragon Nerra had seen who had deliberately killed her foe in such a conflict, cementing her place as the dragon queen.

Naturally, she swooped into the highest, largest spot of them all, settling into place atop a tower while Nerra slid down from her back. Shadr roared her response to the dragons around her, and Nerra found her own mouth shouting along with Shadr, roaring at the same time that Shadr did. The sound seemed to fill the world then, seemed to fill Nerra, until it felt as if there was nothing left of her.

Shadr addressed the dragons then, the power of her mental voice flowing out to the rest of them.

My Chosen and I have gone south. We have seen what there is to see. The time has come now for us to act.

Another dragon, large and with blood red scales, raised its head.

Is the amulet bearer dead, my queen?

Nerra could feel the respect there, the fear. The question was one she could feel hints of around her, but other dragons did not dare to voice it. They were, Nerra realized, terrified of Shadr's power.

We believe the amulet bearer is in the city the human-things call Royalsport, Shadr said. *They have been too cowardly to come out and face us one on one, even when we have killed their people, even one of their princes!*

3

She made it sound like a triumph, as if she hadn't ambushed and murdered Nerra's brother in cold blood. She made it sound as if they hadn't failed at the one thing they'd gone out to do, as if the amulet bearer weren't still there, a danger to them all.

She felt Shadr's disapproval at that thought as much as heard it. She realized too late that so close to the dragon queen, her thoughts were echoing out among the other dragons.

Go down among the Lesser and the Perfected, Shadr commanded her. It was a reprimand of sorts, but the dragon queen framed it as a command. *Relay to them my words. Tell them what I command of all of them. You will be able to feel me.*

Nerra nodded, and then started to descend the black stone of the tower, down a winding staircase that seemed to go on forever, leading her around and around the interior of the place. It had clearly been picked clean by the Lesser and the Perfected, bones lying on the floor where those who had been there had tried to stand against them. Nerra could feel the vial that her brother had given her pressed against her skin as she walked, but she couldn't think about it, because Shadr would order her to destroy even that last remnant of her brother. Nerra forced herself to keep moving, down to street level, out into the black stone square of the inner city.

She walked, and as she walked, she proclaimed the words of the dragon queen, echoing in her head so that to Nerra it felt as if she were a puppet, some hollow shell existing only to be filled with Shadr's voice.

"We tire of waiting," Nerra said. "We have seen the dangers that the human-things pose, and the means that they have to fight against us. They are pitiful, and weak, and will fall easily before the might of flame and claw."

There were Perfected around her now, listening to everything she said as she made her way down toward the gates of the inner city. They were broken open, clearly never to be closed again, and beyond them, the hordes of the Lesser were waiting.

"We will go among them now," Nerra said, or Shadr said through her, she wasn't sure which. "We will claim back what is ours. A group of our kin shall fall upon their strongest city and find the one with the amulet. They shall kill him to clear the way, and slaughter all who stand against us."

4

Nerra could hear the answering voices of the dragons questioning Shadr. They were echoed by some of the Perfected around her, their nerves setting the Lesser into quick, violent movements.

"What about the amulet?" one called out. "If that is still out there, the dragons are in danger?"

"Wasn't the point of you going out with the dragon queen to destroy the amulet bearer?" another asked. "How are we supposed to win if—"

"Silence!" Nerra roared, and she found the sound echoed by one from Shadr, a burst of shadow coming from within the inner city. Again, the dragon queen's words filled her, spilling from her mouth. "Who dares to question the power of Shadr? Who dares to stand against what must be done? It has been commanded, and you will obey!"

In that moment, Nerra understood the tyrant that Shadr was. She was queen only because the others were too afraid to do anything about it. She was a thing of terror and violence, and she would drench the world in blood because of it. Nerra stumbled on, pouring out her words, and yet she knew just how hollow those words were.

There was one side effect of walking as Shadr's emissary to the Perfected like this: with each step, Nerra found that she could feel more of herself and less of the dragon queen. Shadr's voice was still there, but it was a fainter thing now, which didn't threaten to overwhelm everything Nerra was. She could feel her own thoughts there, her own pain, her own grief.

Nerra stumbled with the weight of that grief. She'd had to watch her brother die. She'd been a part of his death, however much she'd tried to hold back from it. She hurt with that knowledge, and she hated Shadr for what she'd done. Gathering her thoughts, she sent the most carefully controlled cluster of them in the direction of the dragon queen.

My queen, I request... I request that before we head south, I be permitted a little time alone to recover. It seems that the exertion of delivering your message has been great.

Shadr's thoughts came back, sharp edged. *You are my Chosen. You should be at my side. You need nothing else.*

Please, my queen, Nerra sent. *Your presence is so overwhelming, so awing. Just a short time to recover.*

Shadr didn't reply for several moments. Nerra suspected that she might be tasting Nerra's thoughts for trickery, but there had been

5

nothing untrue in anything she sent. Shadr was overwhelming, was awe-inspiring, was someone Nerra needed to get away from.

Very well, Shadr said. *A short time. Then we will go south and take what's ours.*

Nerra breathed a sigh of relief, but she knew she didn't have time to stay there and recover. She needed to move. She started to walk, heading away from the city, feeling Shadr's presence in her head receding with every step, until it was a ghost, and then not even that. Until Nerra was left with her grief, her pain, her sense that everything she'd been tied to was something evil.

She started to run.

CHAPTER TWO

Vars walked with the Hidden across their island, feeling his pale skin burning slightly in the sun, his dark hair and loose sailor's clothes whipping in the wind. Fear stalked him with every step, knowing who he was with, and the service he had sworn to them without knowing.

Ahead of him, Verdant stood dressed in petals and vines that shifted around her body as she moved, while her mask covered half of a delicate, almost girlish, face. Void's mask was a blank, giving no clue as to what lay beneath, while his robes seemed to absorb the light, like a hole in the world.

Around Vars, the island seemed to reflect them. There were spaces where greenery rose up, wild and tangled and impossibly alive, trees and flowers seeming to be locked in a desperate fight for light and space until whole areas choked themselves with plant life. Other spaces were clean and austere, marked with symbols that threatened to twist Vars's mind even as he looked at them. There were even places that seemed to run with magma, caught up in fire, although these were fewer now, and seemed to be in the process of being slowly overtaken by the other kinds of spaces.

"You should be happier, Vars," Void said without looking round as they walked.

"I could make him happier," Verdant suggested. "I could run vines into his brain and tweak it just a little, bathe him in the most *beautiful* perfumes."

"And then he would be a broken thing, like the others you have touched," Void replied. It wasn't, Vars realized, that he was the saner of the two; it was simply that his madness was of a hard-edged, cold kind that could pretend at humanity if needed.

And still, Vars followed them both, over broken ground, past spots where impossible flowers bloomed in black and purple. Partly, he did it because he was terrified of them, because he knew the kinds of things that the Hidden could do to someone who angered them. They were sorcerers on a level that could match almost anyone, and the prices

7

they'd paid for power made them even more unpredictable than a normal sorcerer might have been.

Partly, he did it because he had made them a promise. He had sworn allegiance to Verdant, back on the shore of the island he'd washed up on when his ship had been caught in a storm. She'd been wearing the form of a little girl when he did it, and he'd thought it was some game before she went to get help. None of that mattered. Even if she had been under an illusion when he'd sworn his fealty, he could still feel the weight of that obligation pressing down on him, tied there with magic so that if he even thought about stepping away from Verdant, it was like sharp thorns touching his thoughts.

Partly, he did it because there seemed to be the promise of power from them, because they seemed to want something from him and there was still a part of Vars that wanted everything they had to offer.

Partly though, he did it because he simply didn't have anywhere else to go. The ship he'd arrived on sat on the rocks below, slowly being torn apart by the waves and the wind. The people who had come with him were dead or lost. He was exiled from his home, not allowed to return on pain of death. Where else was there for him to be than here?

"You fear us," Void said, pausing in a place where fragments of the air seemed disjointed from one another, refracting the light. It wasn't exactly a question.

"Yes," Vars admitted. It wasn't something he would have admitted earlier in his life. Admitting fear was a kind of admission of weakness, and admitting to weakness sounded like the kind of thing that only a fool would do. Vars had always assumed that his enemies would pounce on any such weakness, because it was exactly what he would have done, and he was never short of enemies, because of how quickly he had always capitalized on such weaknesses.

"You should," Void said.

"People aren't afraid of *me*," Verdant said. She reached down and a flower grew up from the floor. "They love me."

"Because you twist their brains until they do," Void pointed out. He touched the flower and it shattered into pieces.

"I could do that with him too, if you like," Verdant said, in the sweetest of tones. That only made Vars's terror grow.

"Not for now," Void said.

8

Vars found himself thinking of the sailor who had tried to kill him back on the ship. He'd had more than enough reasons to, yet somehow Vars was the one left alive, while the sailor was lost to the ocean. It just went to show how unfair the world was.

"Where are we going?" Vars asked as they continued to walk. The world was starting to lose the unsteadiness that came from having come off a ship, but *he* still felt unsteady, unable to keep up with what was happening to him. He was trying to understand what the Hidden wanted from him, but it was too hard to try to guess.

"Do you think there is no purpose to what we do?" Void asked him, still striding out across the weird, disjointed landscape. There were fractures in that landscape, as if the rocks themselves didn't line up.

"Maybe he thinks we're just taking him for a nice walk?" Verdant said in that too beautiful voice of hers. "Maybe I should show him all my wonderful plants."

"We need him, Verdant," Void said. "You should not be so quick to throw away your toys. Besides, we're almost there."

He gestured, and the air itself seemed to reshape itself, revealing a stone archway that was somehow hidden behind empty space. The archway appeared to be made from black stone, marked with the same mind-twisting symbols as the rest of the island. Void stood on one side of it, and Verdant went to the other, both staring through their masks at Vars.

"You are sworn to Verdant's service, so now we should give you a suitable task, Vars, son of Godwin."

Vars felt his stomach knot in fear. He had no doubt that whatever it was, he wasn't going to like it.

"There's no need to be afraid, sweet one," Verdant said. She seemed to think for a moment. "Actually, there might be a *few*. Especially if you don't do what we tell you. Then there are all the ways I will strip the skin from your bones, and the plants I will grow in you while you still live, the changes I will make to your mind, the ways I will rip pieces off you..."

"I think he has the message," Void said. "I am sure he won't cross us, will you, Vars?"

Vars shook his head hurriedly. He was too afraid to do anything else. The fear seemed to fill him until he overflowed with it. "What... what do you want me to do?"

9

"Nothing that is not to your benefit," Void said. "We have enemies in common. We have the king's sorcerer, you have a family that has exiled you. Together, we have a chance to deal with all of them."

"To deal with all of them?" Vars said, swallowing at the thought of it. His brain raced, trying to keep up with it all.

"To kill them!" Verdant said, clapping her hands together. She looked over at Void. "Is he stupid? You didn't say he was stupid, Void."

"Oh, I'm sure that Vars is very clever indeed," Void said. "Clever enough to understand all the implications of what we are about to do. He will know, for example, that his sister Erin has gone to the Southern Kingdom, and will understand what it means when I tell him that she has been ambushed and defeated by a new pretender to Ravin's throne. His brother Greave, meanwhile, has been struck down by a dragon."

Emotions burst through Vars, shock and grief and pain all flaring through him so quickly that he couldn't keep up with them.

"They... they're..."

"Dead," Verdant said. She seemed to enjoy the word so much that she tried out a few others. "Deceased, defunct, destroyed..."

"No longer an impediment," Void quickly clarified, cutting her off. "Leaving your sister Lenore, the one who banished you, as the only member of your family in the kingdom. The only thing between you and ruling."

This was what they were suggesting? It was a suggestion that made him want to laugh with it, except that doing that would probably get him killed.

"I don't want to be king. I've tried it. The people hated me."

"And do you care what the people think?" Void asked. "What commoners think doesn't matter. *Power* matters. We can give you power. We can lead you to power of your own."

"What do you mean?" Vars asked, because he knew it was what they wanted him to ask.

"A king is supported by his sorcerer," Void said. "With us by your side, you will have more than enough control over your kingdom. But more than that, we are missing a member of our triumvirate. A man of enough ambition could be shown ways to gain power, ways of seeing the world that have nothing to do with petty humanity."

"You're offering to make me one of you?" Vars said.

10

Verdant smiled, while plants wound around her. "It's so wonderful."

"Most people think that sorcery takes some special gift," Void said. "Our foe talks nonsense about balancing forces, about skills carefully learned over decades, or by seeing the world in some special way. But for many willing to pay the right prices, to speak with the right... forces, power is easy to gain."

Vars could only stare at him in the wake of an offer like that. He wanted Vars to become one of the Hidden? It was the kind of possibility that he'd never even contemplated, because how could anyone imagine something like that? Even becoming a king made more sense than that.

"What do you want me to do in return?" he asked, trying to make sense of it.

"Oh, it's so easy," Verdant said. "Something you'll enjoy. Or we'll enjoy. Is there a difference?"

Void, meanwhile, took out a bottle. "This is a substance that turns to gas on contact with air," he explained. "Those who breathe it are unconscious in seconds. Even someone of power will reel from it, weakened and easy to destroy. Enough of it can kill. Use it to slay your sister quietly."

Vars felt sick at the thought. They wanted him to kill Lenore. Even after all he'd done in his life, that thought brought horror with it. Lenore was his sister, his half-sister at least. She'd been the one to spare his life when everyone else had wanted him dead.

"I... I can't," he said.

Instantly, everything was agony for him. It felt as if thorns were being shoved into every inch of his body.

"You can," Verdant said. "You will. You're *ours* now. If you're not going to do what Void wants... well, then I get to have *fun* with you."

Vars could imagine all too easily all the things that Verdant might consider fun.

"You need to kill her to clear the way for yourself," Void said. "But also to draw in Master Grey. We believe he has something we want. We will wait for him in the Great Hall. We will fight him, and then you will use this gas on him while he expends his defenses against us. Verdant and I will slay him. This is what you *will* do."

There was so much certainty in his words that it seemed impossible that Vars might fight the idea. Even so, he tried, standing there until his

11

skin seemed aflame with it, and he felt tears of agony pouring from the corners of his eyes.

"How am I even supposed to get to Royalsport?" he tried. If he could just buy time, find a moment to think, he might be able to find a way out of this, find a way to make this better.

"You're thinking of ways to make this right," Void said. "But what is 'right'? How should the world be, Vars? Should the world be a place where you are a mere peasant, a mere sailor? Should it be a place where every plan you have ever had has come to nothing, and where those who are less than you have come to power?"

"No," Vars said automatically. A part of him that he'd pushed down rose back up then, reminding himself of who he'd been, who he *was*. The world shouldn't be a place where he had no power, where he was reduced to this. He didn't even have Bethe beside him, the way he'd assumed he would.

Void made a gesture with one hand, and the air within the stone arch before him started to shift and shimmer, the image framed by it changing until it was an arch in a courtyard, cobblestones to form a floor, stone walls across from it.

"Getting you where you are meant to be is easy," Void said. "Giving you the tools to do it is easy. Now, you are the one who has to do it. I will make this simple for you, Vars. Kill the queen, slow down the sorcerer, and you will have everything you could ever have wanted. Fail us, and your death will be a thing of nightmares."

Put like that, there was no choice to make. Vars might have pushed down the fears that had controlled him all his life, but those fears were still there under the surface. Perhaps another man might have fought against this, might have had the strength of character to resist the things that were there for the taking.

As it was, instead, Vars stepped up to the shimmering edge of the portal before him, took a breath, and stepped through.

CHAPTER THREE

Lenore dressed with Aurelle's and Orianne's aid. Today, it was one of those days when she needed the help of both of them to fully arrange all the stays of her dress, all the layers of her various garments, into one coherent whole. Her dark hair was already tied up into an elaborate network of braids and curls, some of which contained loops of gold thread, while there was so much powder and paint on her face that she could barely catch a hint of the high cheekbones or full lips beneath.

Around her, the room was filled with gilded ornaments, while high, wide windows provided a view out over the city. The floor was marble, broad enough that a formal dance could have taken place on it, and rugs covered it to warm the feet of those who walked. The bed in one corner was massive and carved. Supposedly, dozens of Lenore's ancestors had slept in it, and Lenore suspected that there was probably space for all of them at once.

"I look like something designed by an architect," Lenore declared, as Orianne settled the crown into place atop her head. Her serving maid was much more simply dressed, in a dark dress that matched the fall of her hair, her slender frame accentuated by it so that she looked like a shadow trailing along behind Lenore.

"You look like a queen," Aurelle corrected her. *She* got to wear hunting gear, complete with gray leather riding britches and a russet doublet. Her deep red hair was tied up out of the way of the strong lines of her face, and if there weren't a dozen knives at her belt, that didn't mean that they weren't there somewhere.

"Like someone's idea of what a queen should be," Lenore corrected her, checking the mirror. The figure staring back at her just didn't look like her, standing there in layers of pale atelier's work until she looked draped in cobwebs. She stood in the middle of her room's gilded opulence, and she looked like too much, far too much.

"That may be the point," Orianne said, with a slight raise of one eyebrow. "Many of the nobles from the dance of suitors have left, but others are staying around."

"They want to see how I perform," Lenore guessed.

13

"Perform being the most important word."

Lenore knew she had a point. All of this was a performance, and she understood the advantages that could come in the royal court from looking one way or another. Look disheveled or out of control, and people might assume that you had no grip on your kingdom. Look like their idea of a powerful queen, and they might be more likely to obey. Even so, Lenore had put up with too much of this in her life.

"No," she said, "this is all wrong. Aurelle, can you fetch me the red and gold dress there, please?"

"Your majesty," Orianne said. "Lord Travers's dressmaker brought this as a gift."

"All the more reason not to wear it," Lenore said. She looked over at Orianne while Aurelle went to fetch the dress. "Orianne, I trust you and I value your opinion, but in this I know what I'm doing. Now, you can either help me out of this… apparatus, or I'll cut myself clear of it. I'm sure Aurelle would lend me a knife."

"She probably would," Orianne said with a sigh, and started to undo the stays trussing Lenore into the thing.

Lenore started to get changed into the much simpler dress Aurelle brought.

"I've told them that I will rule as a queen alone," she said, "but they will still test me, and try to see how far they can push. If I show them *this*…" she started to scrub the layers of powder and paint away, "they will see a queen hemmed in by tradition and formality. They will think that if they find enough scholars, they can find a way to control me with traditions they find, rules I must follow."

She took down the over-elaboration of her hair, keeping it simpler, and setting the crown atop it.

"What queen will they see now?" Lenore asked her reflection.

"The one who told them their dance of suitors was done," Orianne suggested.

"Or perhaps the one who had the pretenders to her throne killed," Aurelle said. "The red will remind them of blood."

Of course she would think of things that way, but maybe she had a point. Maybe the nobles of her court needed that memory kept fresh.

"I have… been thinking about that, my queen," Aurelle said. "Before, I could not go to aid Prince Greave because I was needed to try to stop Finnal and his father. Now, they are dead and…"

14

"You want to go after Greave," Lenore guessed. She knew how much Aurelle cared about her brother. She'd been expecting this almost from the moment Finnal and Duke Viris died.

Aurelle nodded. "I know he wanted me to stay behind, and I know he has his own task to fulfill, but maybe I can help him. Maybe I can be there when he needs me."

"You don't have to justify yourself, Aurelle," Lenore said. "And you don't need my permission to go after Greave. But you have my blessing, both to try to find him and for anything that happens after. Take anything you need."

"Thank you, my queen," Aurelle said, dropping into a curtsey. "I'll find him. I won't let you down."

"You've already done more than anyone could ask," Lenore said. "Go and be happy, Aurelle."

Aurelle hurried off. Lenore hoped that she would find Greave, and that had her thinking of Devin. How long would it be before he was back?

"There," Orianne said. "You look different, at least. Should we head to the Great Hall now, my queen? People will be waiting for you."

Lenore nodded. There was so much still to do, an entire kingdom to run. She walked to the doors of her rooms with Orianne beside her. There were no guards in here, but they would be waiting for her outside, ready to start the procession around the castle that had become her preferred way of doing things, far better than any meeting in the Great Hall could be.

Outside, sure enough, there were the guards, and a waiting crowd of courtiers, all lining the corridors, as much a normal part of them as the tapestries depicting the history of the kingdom, or the statues that were starting to be put back in place to fill the gaps left by the Southern Kingdom's rapaciousness.

A wave of bows and curtseys swept out along the corridor as Lenore stepped out into it, a gap left for her to walk to the front of this procession, the court starting to get used to the way she preferred to do things now. Lenore paused here and there as she went along, stopping to touch a hand or offer a smile.

"How is your family?" she asked a servant.

"Well, my queen," the man replied.

She paused at one of the lords there. "It is good to see that you remained after the dance of suitors, Lord Hellas."

15

"Well, I never really stood a chance," the man said. "Although some of the others are licking their wounds in the country."

"I'm sure they will return," Lenore said. Actually, she filed it away as one more thing to check on, making sure that the country would continue to run smoothly. There were so many others to deal with, but she knew by now that was what being queen was: being the one who ultimately had to make the decisions others didn't want to.

She started the procession through the castle, down one of the winding staircases, along a gallery with a checkerboard floor. They started to come forward to her one by one: the servants and the scholars, the peasants and the nobles. Everyone who had an issue they thought the queen could solve came forward, and because Lenore was walking, there were no carefully delineated squares for each rank of the nobility and lesser folk to determine which order they got to speak to her in. Instead, they came to her almost randomly, small issues mixed in with great ones: a woman hoped that her husband had been found among the dead, a noble alleged that his lands had been encroached on by another as the Southern Kingdom's forces receded.

Lenore dealt with the requests one by one, mostly passing people off to those officials of her court who had the knowledge and expertise to help them. By now, at least those officials had come to learn how Lenore's reign worked, and they were waiting close by to move off with the petitioners as Lenore called for their assistance.

It was all going smoothly until they reached the Great Hall. The doors there were open, and a single figure was standing within the vastness of it, leaning on a staff of twisted wood and wearing robes of white, trimmed with gold. It was an impressive sight, even for Lenore.

"Master Grey," Lenore said. She held up a hand, and the procession behind her stopped. "Orianne, with me."

She walked forward and shut the doors behind her, leaving her, Orianne, and the sorcerer alone in the hall together. It was strange being in here without people, the banners of the kingdom fluttering blue and gold around them, the throne sitting empty at one end of the cavernous space. Master Grey was standing at the exact center of it all, waiting for them.

Lenore walked forward to him with Orianne at her side.

"Impressive," Master Grey said.

"What is?" Lenore asked.

"That your people obey your smallest gesture," Master Grey said. "You have started to become the ruler that you could be."

If Lenore had been less worried, she might have taken the time to appreciate that compliment.

"What is it?" she asked. "Is it Devin?"

That was the first place that her mind went, because of course Master Grey would tell her if something happened to his apprentice, wouldn't he? Fear filled Lenore as she waited for the answer, then relief as Master Grey shook his head.

"I have no news of what has happened to my apprentice, but the news I do have is graver still."

Lenore tried to believe that there could be news worse than something happening to Devin. She forced herself to keep listening.

"I believe that the other young man I sent with him, Anders, has an artifact of great power," Master Grey said. "I have sent... someone after them, but the danger it represents is considerable. It is an amulet that allows for control of dragons."

Lenore heard Orianne gasp at that news, and she couldn't blame her maidservant. Something like that was a lot to take in.

"This might have been useful to know when there were dragons attacking the city," Lenore said.

"The Southern Kingdom controlled it at the time," Master Grey pointed out. "And I thought I had control of the amulet. We must focus on the danger at hand. The young man, Anders, has stolen it, and I believe that means that dragons will be coming to the city in force. They held back only because if its threat, and now they will be coming."

Lenore tried to imagine what that might mean. It was hard, though, to imagine whole flights of dragons swooping down on the city, flame coming from every direction. The thought of it brought fear, for herself, for her city, for her whole kingdom.

"How do we stop an army of them," she asked, "when one almost burned down the city?"

"I still have hopes," Master Grey said. "I believe that Devin may yet make a difference, but I felt that I needed to prepare you for the danger. We need to be ready for the possibility that dragons will reach the city, bringing with them other creatures, things that are humanlike, but bestial."

For a moment, Lenore couldn't think, couldn't take it all in. She'd thought that they had time, and that the plans they'd put in place would be enough. Now... now there were dragons coming for the city and she wasn't sure what to do.

Except she was queen, and she didn't have the *luxury* of not knowing.

"Orianne, open the doors and let people in. Bring me the captain of the guards, and as many of the nobles who have command over forces as you can find. Bring me engineers from the House of Scholars. I want to know if they can produce weapons that might harm a dragon. Start to bring food inside the city. If we have to bring people inside the walls to keep them safe, I want to know that they can be fed."

She rattled off the orders, and quickly, Orianne was opening the doors to the Great Hall. Lenore looked around to find Master Grey staring at her.

"What?" she asked.

"Simply that of all of the ones who could have ruled at this moment, I am glad that it is you," Master Grey said. Lenore heard him sigh. "I just hope that it will be enough."

CHAPTER FOUR

Erin worked on the bonds that held her as the palanquin bounced its way back toward Sandport, its cushions absorbing some of the jolting, its wooden frame a solid square around her. Her muscles worked against the ropes, and she fought to show no sign of her frustration as she did it, not with Nicholas St. Geste staring over at her.

He sat there, dark hair falling around the bronze skin of his face, pale silks wrapped around broad shoulders and a muscular frame. He had a backwards curved blade sitting across his knees.

"What?" she demanded. "Trying to decide if you should kill me?"

"Yes," he said. "I just hadn't expected the person the Northern Kingdom sent to kill me to be so..."

"So *what*?" Erin demanded.

Nicholas shrugged. "So pretty."

That took Erin a little aback. People called Lenore pretty, not her. She was the one who was too short, who looked almost like a boy, who hacked her hair back so that it wouldn't get in the way if she had to fight. Her dark eyes locked on him, sure that this was some kind of joke.

"If you like me so much, you could let me go," Erin suggested. "Or is that not how you do things here? Maybe you've decided to just carry me off."

"Or maybe I want to keep the person who came to kill me and destroy my country safe where she couldn't do any harm," Nicholas shot back. "Don't think I've forgotten what you're here for."

"What *I'm* here for?" Erin snapped back, anger rising in her. "You're trying to put the Southern Kingdom together. You're trying to be a new Ravin!"

"And you're trying to tear it all apart! Do you know how bad things have been without a strong leader here?" Nicholas snapped back. "You want us weak so that you can control us. You want to invade and run the world for your own benefit."

"You killed my friends!" Erin shouted, and in the small space of the conveyance, it seemed too loud.

19

All her friends, dead. She'd brought a dozen companions with her to the Southern Kingdom, and now they were gone. Some had died along the way, from the violence of the kingdom, or simply from its harshness. And others had perished when she'd led them into the ambush. Erin could still remember Ceris the archer stumbling from the shadows, a knife sticking from her back.

If she could have gotten clear, she would have killed Nicholas then, would have taken that sword from him and run it through his chest. The only problem with that was that the last time she'd tried that, she and Nicholas had ended up knocking one another unconscious.

"Why send you?" Nicholas asked Erin. "Why send the sister of the northern pretender?"

"Lenore's no pretender!" Erin snapped. "She took her throne back from a monster! From a man who slaughtered our people and murdered my mother!"

"Who held the kingdom together," Nicholas shot back. "Who stopped warlords from fighting among themselves, trying to control every corner. They tell me that you saw Inedrin. Do you want someone like *him* running the Southern Kingdom?"

"I don't want *anyone* running it," Erin said.

"So you'd rather have chaos and violence?" Nicholas demanded.

"If it keeps my people safe!" Erin shouted at him.

"And damn *mine*?" Nicholas said. "Typical arrogant northerner. Only your people matter. Only your people have the right to live and to be happy."

Erin looked away from him, but another flare of anger made her look back again. "You *killed* my people. You're nothing more than a butcher."

Nicholas sat in silence for several seconds, and for a moment, Erin thought that perhaps she'd gone too far. When he lifted the sword, she was all but certain of it. She braced herself, thinking of her sister, her brother. How would they react when she didn't come back? How much more pain could there be for one family?

The sword swept around, and Erin braced herself for its impact, determined not to show this would-be tyrant any fear, even as he murdered her. Then the sword sliced through the ropes holding her legs, and Erin groaned as she was able to move again.

"Come with me," Nicholas said, and slipped from the palanquin.

20

Erin followed in his wake for the first couple of steps, down onto the track that led through the sandy wastes. There were dunes on every side, and the whisper of the wind made sand tumble from them.

She found herself in the middle of a column of troops marching together in what Erin assumed was the direction of Sandport. Erin saw the wise woman there who had directed them toward the ambush, walking with the others, obviously one of them. She was covered in charms and shifting layers of cloth, so that it took a moment to realize that she was younger than she seemed.

"You have met Ankari," Nicholas said. "She is one of those I trust the most." He gestured to another man, his dark skin marked with white paint, who wore the kind of robes designed to keep off sand that Erin had worn to pass unnoticed through the kingdom. "And this is Sarit."

"Do you think I *care* about meeting your little crew of killers?" Erin demanded.

"No, of course not," Nicholas said. "You don't care about anyone except—"

Erin chose that moment to run, between one word and the next, plunging into a gap between two of Nicholas's guards and shoving one aside as she ran for the sands. With her arms still bound, there was no chance to grab a weapon and do what she wanted to do: to finish off this would-be Ravin. Still, she could run, and get to safety. Then she could come back and finish this in her own time.

Erin plunged into the dark blindly, tripping and rising and tripping again. Sand gave way beneath her feet, while after her, shouts came from the men following her.

"You can't run!" Nicholas called. "You think you can lose *us* in the sand?"

By day, he might have had a point. Erin had no doubt that she was leaving tracks that a blind man could follow. Even they couldn't hope to follow her like this, with only the first glimmers of dawn light turning the horizon red. She changed directions at random, determined to lose her pursuers.

Erin found a spot in the sand to settle down, huddling in place and covering herself with the robes she wore while she worked on the bonds that still held her arms. She felt them start to loosen, little by little, until at last she was able to free her hands. She wrapped the rope around her fists. A strangling rope wasn't much of a weapon, but it was better than nothing.

21

Erin knew that she should probably get as far away from the caravan as possible, but if she did that, she might never get another chance to kill Nicholas St. Geste. He would go back to Sandport, and getting to him there, when she was alone, would be far too difficult.

So instead, she started to creep back in the direction of the palanquin, staying low, no more than another shadow among the many before the dawn. Erin could hear the sounds of people searching further out in the desert, coordinating with each other using shouts and whistles while Erin slipped closer to the space between them all where she hoped Nicholas St. Geste would be.

She crept up the side of a dune, heading toward the track the palanquin had been traveling along. Below, she could see people spread out, a small number of guards there around Nicholas, along with that wise woman who had tricked her so thoroughly. She would die too, if Erin got the chance.

Then she saw the other figures there, barely identifiable by the growing light. Erin froze in place, making out the forms of Sarel and Yannis, Ulf and Bertram, even Nadir, standing sullenly at the end. She stared at them, not able to believe it. She'd been so sure that they were dead. She'd seen Ceris die in front of her and she'd been so sure that they'd slaughtered all of them. She'd been certain that she was the last one left alive, and that the others were just bones left in the desert.

Erin stared at all of them, trying to work out what to do. They looked bruised, and were tied together on a long rope, their weapons taken from them, their hands bound before them.

Erin's mind raced, trying to work out what was going on, trying to work out the best way to help the people she'd brought with her. Emotions ran through her in a torrent: relief that they were still alive, shock that they were there in front of her, fear of what might happen to them next. She'd brought them here, had been responsible for them, had been the one who had led them straight to what she'd thought were their deaths. She'd thought that she'd failed them as thoroughly as it was possible for a leader to fail those with her.

Now, she had a second chance, and she couldn't fail them again. She had to find a way to save them.

"I know that you are out there," Nicholas called out into the dawn. He stood there among Erin's crew with that blade of his held loosely in his hand. Was it a coincidence that he was facing the same direction

22

where she was hiding? From here, it seemed as if he was staring up into her soul, able to see through her attempts at deception easily.

"I heard the hate in your voice," Nicholas said. "You want to kill me too much to simply run. You're trying to think of all the ways that you might still get down here to do the Northern Kingdom's dirty work."

Erin wanted to shout down that he knew nothing about her, except... well, she *had* been creeping closer to try to find a way to kill him.

"The ones who came with you are here," Nicholas called up. "My guess is that you want to save them, too. So let me tell you the best way to do that, invader: come down now. Give yourself up. You're out there with no water and no food, no way to do what you came to do. Come down."

Erin ignored his words at first. Of course a man like him would threaten the people with her, standing there with his weapon bared, the threat of it implicit. If she didn't come down there, what would he do? Start cutting pieces off the people who had trusted her? Start killing them, one by one, until she did what he wanted?

Erin thought of all the stories she had heard about Nicholas St. Geste and she knew that he would do all of that and more. She knew something else, too: she couldn't let that happen. She'd thought that she'd gotten them killed once. She knew that if she didn't go down there, it was going to happen again. There was only one way to stop that.

"I'm here," she said, standing up and starting to walk down toward him. Briefly, she wondered if there might be a chance to do something even now, if it might be possible to charge him and strike him down while he still thought that she was surrendering.

That chance didn't happen, though, because Nicholas's men moved to intercept her even as she approached. They tied Erin's hands again, adding her to the end of the line that held her friends.

"Don't try to run again," Nicholas said, in a tone that promised things would get worse if she tried. "You are going to Sandport, whether you like it or not."

He moved off to call his guards back, leaving Erin behind like she didn't matter. That was the strangest part of all of this. All she'd heard told Erin that Nicholas St. Geste was a monster, so why hadn't he finished this already?

Why hadn't he killed her?

CHAPTER FIVE

Anders hunted the ancient dragon by feel across the landscape. The amulet he wore pulsed to him with power, leading him toward it as surely as the trail of destruction that it had wrought. He rode after it, dark cloak streaming behind him, dark leathers keeping off the rain that started to fall. That rain streaked across strong features, and slicked back the blond of his hair. He had to hunch over his muscular frame in the saddle to keep riding, but he didn't slow or stop. This was too important for that.

A part of him wished that he'd been able to climb down into the fissure to retrieve the sword Devin had made. *Loss* had been a powerful weapon, and Anders would have liked it in his hand when he went to confront Master Grey. At the very least, it might have been good to lay his would-be rival's body to rest, perhaps to burn it with the same magic he had such a weak grasp of compared to Anders.

None of that truly mattered now, though. The amulet around Anders's neck was enough. The power in it promised true control of dragons, and even the queen's sorcerer couldn't hope to stand against that. Anders just had to keep riding, and he would have a weapon that made a mere sword look like a child's toy by comparison.

He came to a village, and just from the people standing in the streets before their thatched houses, he could tell that the dragon had been by this way. They had the terrified look of folk who had seen something beyond their comprehension.

Their village showed signs of the dragon's passing, too. One of the houses seemed unnaturally frozen, and Anders had already seen the things that the ancient dragon's breath could do. A large spattering of blood on the ground suggested the spot where a cow or a sheep had been snatched up. At least, Anders hoped that it was a farm animal.

"The dragon came this way?" he called out to one of the villagers there, a woman who dropped into a curtsey as he approached.

"Yes, my lord," the woman said.

"Which way did it go?" Anders demanded. The sooner he caught up to it, the sooner he would be able to destroy Master Grey, the way he had his precious student.

The woman pointed east, and Anders started off in that direction. He'd only gone a short distance when a group of men moved to block the way. There were almost half a dozen of them, standing there with makeshift weapons, mostly knives and axes. Two had bows, so Anders dropped down from his horse, ready for trouble.

"There is no need for violence here," he said.

"No?" one of the men said. "We'll decide that, stranger. A beast like that comes to our village, and now you're here asking after it? Seems like those two things might be connected."

"I'm hunting the creature," Anders said. "And every moment you slow me down is one in which it might strike somewhere else."

"That, or you brought it down on us, and you're here to see the results of what you've done," the peasant said.

"I've told you what I'm about," Anders replied. "I am the one chosen to stop the dragons. Now step aside. I will not ask again."

"Oh, it's threats now, is it?" the man said. "And all this about being some chosen one?"

He took a step forward.

Anders had put up with enough. Devin had showed him conclusively that giving peasants ideas above their station never worked out well. Better to teach these men a lesson. So he did.

He raised a hand and used a fragment of magic to snap the bow strings, the tension on them releasing suddenly, sending them snapping out into the faces of the men who held them. One of the axe men came in at Anders and he stepped in to meet him, throwing him smoothly over his hip. His sword was out then, coming up to slice into the torso of the next man to come at him. The crowd of them fell back in obvious fear.

"Sorcerer!" one called out. They turned and ran then. Those who could, at least. The one Anders had struck down with his sword lay unmoving. One look told Anders that he would never rise again. Perhaps once, before he had lost so many people on the quests the sorcerer had set him, that might have troubled Anders.

Anders walked to retrieve his horse. The young woman who had pointed the way before stood near it, edging back away from him.

26

"Please," she begged. "Please don't hurt me. I'll do anything you want."

"Why would I want anything from you?"

He didn't want her fear. He'd *told* them all why he was there, and they still hadn't listened. The woman was crying now, for no reason Anders could understand. Anders ignored her and got back on his horse. She didn't matter. It was just one of the truths he'd learned in all this.

He rode from the village, heading in the direction she'd pointed. There was a stream there, which Anders forded, and a long track leading out across scattered hills. He thought as he rode, about the lessons Master Grey had obviously tried to teach him, and about the ones he actually had. He'd betrayed Anders when he'd trained Devin alongside him without ever letting him know, when he'd allowed Anders's childhood to be swept up in preparation for a destiny that hadn't even been settled on one person. He'd said that Anders and Devin were needed together, but Anders had ended that the moment he'd kicked Devin into the fissure.

That was the first lesson: there was no destiny, only what you made happen.

The second lesson had come when Master Grey had shut him inside the walls of his tower: for the truly powerful, there were no rules, because there was no one to stop them.

The third… well, the third came in Master Grey's manipulations, but also in every glance around this world, at people such as the ones who had tried to slow Anders down in the village. They were less than him, simply *less*, in every way. They didn't have a fraction of his training, or skill, or natural gifts. Compared to him, they were as stupid as sheep in a field. The lesson was simple: since there was no one else as worthy, it fell to him to decide things for everyone else.

For one brief moment, it seemed to Anders that he actually understood the way that Master Grey thought. There was no doubting that the sorcerer was powerful, so why *shouldn't* he decide things for everyone else?

The only question now was what Anders wanted. Revenge on Master Grey, obviously, because after all he'd done, he didn't deserve to come out of this in one piece. After that though, what?

Anders realized with a start that the answer was essentially what he had always wanted: he wanted to truly be the chosen one. Given the things he'd learned about the world, that seemed difficult, but he wanted it nonetheless. He wanted to be the one who saved them all from the dragons. He wanted the adulation that came from that and the position. He wanted to sweep into Royalsport and everyone there to bow down to him in awe at what he'd done.

Anders found himself thinking about all the rewards he'd dreamed of as a boy, all the things that he'd simply assumed would flow from being chosen for this, but which had slowly ebbed away as the truth of the magus's manipulations had shown itself. He'd assumed that there would be wealth, that he would have a position of power, that the king might even marry him to one of his daughters.

Anders decided there and then that he would have all of that. He would make sure of it. He would return as the one who saved them all, and he would have everything that came from it, including Queen Lenore. They would give it to him, or he would *take* what he deserved.

Anders was still thinking about the possibilities when he felt the pull of the amulet change. Before, the ancient dragon had been the only thing he could feel, its presence ahead of him as sure and certain as the sun moving across the sky. Now, though, he could feel something else. Something… bigger.

Anders didn't know what to make of it until he rode hard to the top of a hill and paused there, looking out. He strained his eyes as he watched the horizon, looking in the direction that the amulet was now pulling him in. He saw the city there, Astare sitting in the distance, with dots in the sky above it, and at first he thought that he might simply be looking at a flock of birds.

It was a moment or two before he realized that it was a flock of *dragons*. They wheeled over the remains of the city on broad wings, huge, scaled reptiles of every color moving in a wedge of might and power. Below them, humanoid creatures teemed, in a swarm that seemed to cover the land, filling the space where the city had once been. The city itself lay in ruins, torn apart by their hands, and for several seconds Anders could only stare at it.

Looking at them there, Anders felt almost ashamed that he'd thought that one old, weakened dragon would be enough to control everything. Compared to what he could see on the horizon, that was nothing. This… this was an army of dragons.

28

For the briefest instant, Anders knew fear at the sight of so many of them. How could humanity hope to stand against something like that? How could anyone possibly hope to defeat all of them?

Then he realized that he was still thinking like the man Master Grey had wanted him to be. He was still thinking like he had to take them on, fight them, win against them. Anders didn't need to do that; he needed to control them. The only question was whether the amulet would give him enough power to do that.

No, he didn't even need to do that. If he wanted to control a country, he wouldn't seek to control every person in it; if he wanted to control the direction of an army, he wouldn't speak to each soldier. That was one lesson Master Grey *had* taught him: apply force in the right place and one could achieve miracles.

Here, it was easy to see where the spot was to apply force: a great black dragon flew over the city, larger than any of the others, a corona of shadow seeming to follow it as it flew. Anders had learned enough about dragons to recognize one that held power among them. All the old stories talked of them having queens, strong enough to hold their place against any challenger, able to command their kin as surely as a human queen might command her kingdom.

If he could get close to that one, Anders knew that he would have more power than he could ever have dreamed of. The amulet would give him power over the dragon queen, and through her, he would be able to gain control of all the dragons that followed in her wake. He wouldn't just have a dragon; he would control an army.

CHAPTER SIX

For Renard, tracking the path the dragon had taken wasn't hard. He was a man who could follow a mark across a city's roofs, find a soon to be stolen treasure in the dark, or simply locate all of his clothes before an angry suitor came back. He and Devin simply followed the trail of destruction it had left in the landscape, the ice and the burn marks, the torn up trees and the damaged buildings.

"Do you think we'll catch up to it soon?" he asked Devin, then took a second look at him and asked the more important question. "Are you doing all right?"

"I'll live," Devin said. To Renard's eyes, though, he looked pretty beaten up, his broad frame bruised and battered, his dark hair carrying flecks of blood from falling into the fissure. His traveling clothes were stained with blood too, but that was from where they'd buried his slain wolf so that predators couldn't eat it. He had a determined set to his features that Renard knew well, largely because a few men had come at him with that expression: it was the look of a man with someone to kill. One hand rested on the hilt of a sword whose blade looked fancy and rune encrusted, yet whose hilt was made of simple materials, the kind of things that might have been scavenged somewhere.

"Tell me more about the amulet," Devin said as they followed in the wake of the dragon.

Renard was a bit worried about telling him all of it. After all, he'd seen how eager the Hidden were for it, and then presumably this Anders. If anyone understood the all too human urge to divest the world of precious things, it was Renard.

"Tell me," Devin repeated. "Please. I need to know how dangerous it is."

On the other hand, Devin was almost certainly on his side, and he was also in the kind of mood where it probably wasn't a good idea to antagonize him. More than that, Master Grey had sent Renard after Devin specifically for this. If Renard couldn't trust him, who could he trust?

"The amulet was designed to give the wearer power over dragons," he said. "But it only works for those it recognizes as 'worthy' somehow, because the sorcerer who created it didn't want it falling into the wrong hands."

"I think it's a bit late for that," Devin said, as they continued over broken ground, heading east.

"To be honest, Master Grey thought that it mostly recognizes power," Renard said. "Well, that and anyone with enough of the right bloodline. I carried that damn thing for *days*."

He could remember the weakness that had come from it. He had no desire to feel that again, but it still seemed better than the amulet being in the hands of a man like Anders. Gods, how much trouble was the world in when Renard was the safest pair of hands for something like that?

A village lay ahead, and the people of it stared at him and Devin as they passed through it. Renard saw the spot where a body had been dragged to the side of the road, and a couple of people had bruises like they'd been in a fight.

"Did someone come through here?" Devin asked. "A young man my age, in dark clothes?"

A young woman there just pointed silently.

"You friends of his?" one of the men asked, and for a moment Renard wondered if they might have walked into trouble.

Then Devin looked around, fixing him with a stare. "No."

They backed off. In the face of that stare from Devin, Renard would have too. He quietly resolved not to be too close by when they finally caught up to Anders. He stayed by Devin's side, though, knowing that some things were too important for him to walk away from.

"You know we're heading for Astare?" Renard said, as they kept walking east. "If we keep going long enough, we're going to hit the coast, and from what I've heard, that's where the dragons are."

"It's going to rejoin its kind," Devin said. He sounded bothered by it, but not as bothered as Renard was, which was to say that he didn't stop and turn away from the nest of dragons that they were walking into.

"What I'm saying is that there's only so far we can follow this dragon before we run into a lot of other dragons," Renard pointed out. Even that didn't seem to do the trick.

"We'll reach it before then," Devin said.

31

Renard frowned slightly. "Um… is that actually *better*? Master Grey sent me to find you, and try to help get the amulet away from Anders. He didn't say anything about chasing after dragons."

"He sent *me* to try to connect with the dragon who bonded with the original magus," Devin said. "I've not given up on that."

"After all Anders has done, you're still trying to save the kingdom?" Renard asked, a little surprised by it. Oh, he'd played up his own heroic acts before now, but this actually *was* heroic. To forgo revenge in order to do the right thing was… well, it was kind of impressive.

"The people I care about are still in danger," Devin said.

"And I guess it can't hurt to have a dragon on your side when you go after Anders?" Renard guessed. They said that revenge was best served cold, so maybe the ice of the ancient dragon's breath would do the trick. "Of course, first we have to… catch it."

Renard trailed off because of *course* that was the moment when the great bulk of the ancient dragon came into view ahead, grounded in a field, wings spread as if stretching them out in the sun.

It was huge on a scale Renard could barely comprehend, its white bulk graying with age, so that it looked like a huge snow mound in the middle of the field. The sun gleamed from it, and fragments of ice fell from its skin. When its wings spread, they were like the sails of a windmill there, filling the field. Its neck stretched up, sinuous and snakelike, flexing this way and that with great, catlike eyes blinking in the sun. It opened its mouth wide and a gout of flame went up into the sky, changing to ice halfway through, so that the two hit one another and rain came down over the field in a sudden burst. Renard thought he'd seen everything there was from dragons with the ones he'd met before. This one though… a sense of awe briefly rose in him at the sight.

The dragon itself looked strangely tired, moving sluggishly, stretching itself in the sun to try to get as much of it on its skin as it could. Renard guessed that its bulk meant that it needed more of the warmth of the sun to heat itself than any smaller lizard would have, and if it was anything like its much smaller kin, that would mean that it was much slower than it would otherwise have been.

"The flight must have worn it out," Devin said beside Renard.

"The size of it, I'm not surprised," Renard said.

32

Devin shook his head. "With the dragons I've seen before, it hasn't been like this. They've been more agile."

Renard thought back to the ones that had almost killed him in his time as the bearer of the amulet. Those had been agile in spite of their size, able to move in the air with all the speed and control of something much smaller. He distinctly remembered the one that had come for him outside of Geertstown hovering there before him, holding in place while it tried to work out whether to burn him alive or not.

"Is there something wrong with it?" Renard asked, and then cursed himself for even asking it. The gods took enough amusement with him without giving them obvious opportunities. Questioning something that seemed to be going well wasn't what you did. If life as a thief and then as a celebrated hero of Royalsport had taught him anything, it was that you needed to take advantage of situations while you could.

"I don't know," Devin said. "It's ancient. Master Grey said that it was old even before it froze itself at the heart of the volcano. It did that so it could survive for when it was needed again, but now..." He paused, considering the dragon. "I think it's old. I think it's dying."

"That doesn't sound like a good thing," Renard pointed out. "From what you said about bonding with it, it dying probably isn't going to help."

"So long as I'm connected to it long enough to stop the dragons from slaughtering Royalsport," Devin said. "We have to try, at least."

"Okay," Renard said. "Um... are you sure you can do this?"

What Renard would have liked was for his traveling companion to immediately come back with a declaration of certainty, for Devin to tell him that all of this was just a formality, or that better yet, Renard should stand back and leave him to it. As it was, he stood there far too long.

Renard sighed. "All right. How close do you need to be?"

"Why?" Devin asked.

"Because *obviously* I'm the distraction," Renard said. "Just *try* to connect to it, or whatever you're doing, before it kills me."

"You're going to go and try to distract it?" Devin said. He sounded slightly shocked.

"I know. I liked life better when I wasn't trying to be a hero, too," Renard said. "If... if this goes wrong, tell Meredith... I don't know. Make something up."

33

He steeled himself and strode forward, drawing his sword, trying not to think about what a stupid idea this was. He didn't show a trace of fear, but that was only because he'd always been a good actor. Inside, he was shaking.. When he got closer, he started to do the one thing he *knew* would manage to distract anything: he sang.

"There once was a girl from Astare, who found fame both near and afar..."

Renard would have preferred it to be something heroic, "The Song of Alar" or "The Ballad of the Three Battles," perhaps. As it was, it seemed like he was about to go to his death armed with nothing more than a sword and a handful of ribald lyrics.

The dragon turned its head toward him, staring at him... well, not unlike one or two of his previous audiences, to be honest. It was the mixture of disbelief, anger, and simple desire to get away that Renard thought he recognized.

"That's it," he said. "Look at me. All your attention right on..."

He flung himself to the side as a burst of flame hit the ground where he'd been standing. Renard rolled to his feet, dodged a swipe of claws, and kept moving. *This* was slow and old? He barely dodged a burst of frost, and the worst part was that he couldn't strike back, or even run; he had to keep the distraction going.

"That's it," Renard said. "This way. I'm right here."

He stood there for a second, taunting the dragon, and that was when its wing whipped round, hitting him with the force of a charging horse. The impact battered Renard from his feet, sending him sprawling so that for several seconds all he could do was stare upwards, the world spinning around him.

The dragon reared over him, looking down at him in something between confusion and contempt. It lifted a claw, and the sunlight caught it, sharp and pointed, like a sword poised over his heart. Renard tried to roll out of the way, but for the moment, everything hurt too much to even move. All he could do was stare up at the claw that was going to kill him, unable to even begin to avoid it.

The claw seemed to hang there above him forever. Renard had time to think of everything he would be leaving behind, and there was depressingly little of it. A few people who would remember his name for a while, perhaps Meredith would be sad if she heard about this, or simply annoyed at him if he didn't come back...

34

Slowly, it dawned on Renard that it didn't just *seem* like a long time since the dragon had raised its clawed foot over him. It stood poised there, but it wasn't making any move to kill him. Instead, its head was slowly moving around, staring at the spot where Renard realized that Devin stood. It locked eyes with Devin, and for several seconds Renard had the feeling that there was a power passing between them that Renard couldn't understand.

Very carefully, Renard rolled out from underneath the bulk of the dragon and stood.

"It's all right," Devin said. "We… I can feel the connection."

"So, you're joined to the dragon?" Renard asked.

Devin nodded. "I can feel everything it is, everything it was. I can see its memories of the sorcerer."

"And does that mean you can stop all the *other* dragons from burning down the world?" Renard asked.

"I don't know," Devin admitted.

"And Anders?"

Devin's expression looked almost as impossible to read as the dragon's in that moment.

"Now we find him, and we end this."

CHAPTER SEVEN

Aurelle was riding over open farmland when she saw all the signs of an ambush: wheat that rustled against the direction of the wind, silence where there should have been the small sounds of birds or animals, even just a sense that there was something wrong. Aurelle had learned to trust her instincts, and now they were telling her that there was someone, or some*thing*, there.

She rode forward slowly; her quest was too important to turn back. At every village she'd passed, Aurelle asked after Greave, her need to find him making the words spill out over one another as she described him, desperate to be certain about the direction in which he'd gone. Those delicate, almost feminine features were easy enough to describe, and it seemed that plenty of villagers recognized them, because several pointed the way.

Aurelle kept her horse moving forward, certain now that someone was watching. Aurelle didn't want to think about what they saw when they looked at her, or what the villagers thought. Some red-haired, slender woman of the court in fine traveling clothes, chasing after a lover who had jilted her, perhaps. Some courtesan chasing after a patron who had become far more? Some assassin seeking out the one she'd been sent for?

There were times when all of those might have applied. Aurelle's relationship with Greave had been so complicated that by normal standards it probably barely counted as one. Yet there had never been anyone else Aurelle had loved in the same way.

Her eyes scanned the fields around her, looking over the dry stone walls, the wheat and barley. There still wasn't any movement there, but Aurelle didn't need movement to be certain, and she wasn't going to turn back. Greave mattered too much.

Everyone else who had been her lover, her patron, her friend or anything else to her had always wanted something from her, had always found a way to use her, or had been there because Aurelle wanted that, whether it was information, money, or their death.

She'd tracked Greave. Now, she was in the middle of nowhere, and someone was out to ambush her.

"I know you're there," Aurelle said. She drew out a long knife. "Come out."

Instead, there was a rustle in the undergrowth, as whatever was there moved away from her. Aurelle dismounted her horse and moved to intercept that movement. It occurred to her that she might be stalking some lost sheep, broken out from an enclosure. Every instinct she had told her that it *wasn't* anything like that, though. This was something dangerous, something she couldn't just ride past.

The creature that came out of the field definitely wasn't a sheep. It was human-sized but lizard-like, with deep blue scales that seemed to shine with hints of other colors as the light hit them. It had a pointed snout, and a long tail that emerged, incongruously, from beneath the hem of a pale robe. Its hands featured long claws that seemed as sharp as any knife, but the most disturbing part was the eyes, which seemed to have something almost humanlike about them.

The shock of seeing the thing there was so great that Aurelle lashed out automatically. It was important never to hesitate in a fight. Once the decision had been made that something was a threat, it was better to kill it before it could strike back. Aurelle's knife snaked out with all the speed and strength she could muster, but it still only skittered from armored scales as the creature in front of her twisted away from her.

"Wait!" the creature said, but Aurelle knew better than to wait just because an enemy told her to. She struck out again, aiming for her foe's throat.

The creature caught her arm in midair, simple strength arresting the movement. It was one of those things that people who had never been in a knife fight thought was easy, but to do it to someone like Aurelle, who kept her weapon moving and was careful not to leave her arm hanging where it might be struck? Doing it required an inhuman level of speed.

"I don't want to hurt you," the creature said. Its voice was as incongruous as its eyes, sounding human in a way that should never have come from anything that looked like that. It sounded like a human girl, speaking with the accent of the Northern Kingdom.

It threw Aurelle away, her knife clattering to the ground as Aurelle slammed down into the dirt, hard enough to take the breath out of her. That voice though... *that* shocked Aurelle more. She had heard about the creature that Greave had gone off hunting, the one that had been able to speak to people during the attacks by the dragon. She had heard who it claimed to be.

"Princess Nerra?" Aurelle said.

"Yes. It's Aurelle, isn't it? I remember you from court." Even though the creature said it, it was still hard for Aurelle to believe that this had ever been human, ever been the princess. She stood there over Aurelle, watching her with movements that had nothing human in them, and Aurelle had to work hard to accept that this could be the princess, that this could be who Greave had been chasing after.

What was the alternative, though? Try to kill her again? She'd already shown that Aurelle had almost no chance of making that work in any kind of head on fight. Maybe if she had the advantage of surprise, or was able to shoot from a distance, but otherwise, it was simply suicide.

This creature knew her. There was only one way for that to happen that Aurelle could think of: she was telling the truth.

"What... what are you doing here?" Aurelle said, trying to work out what was going on.

"I ran away," Nerra said. "Shadr, the dragon queen, she's gone too far. When she's close, I can feel her in my head. I had to get clear after everything she's done."

"What?" Aurelle said. Normally, she was good at making sense of complex, shifting events, but this was too much, too quickly. She'd barely begun to accept that this might possibly be Princess Nerra, but now, it seemed that there were far more things that Aurelle had to make sense of.

"I should tell you all of it," Nerra—and Aurelle could accept it was her now—said. "I remember that you were Greave's... that you and he..." She stopped for a moment, and Aurelle thought she saw a look of pain on the creature's face. "There are things that I have to tell you. There's something you need to know."

She led Aurelle over to one of the low stone walls that lined the field. They sat on it together, and it might have seemed almost normal if Aurelle's horse hadn't been shying away from the presence of this lizard creature who was also somehow a princess.

"I fled from Shadr," Nerra said. "Shadr is the queen of the dragons, the strongest of them. They follow her, and she wants to either return human-things to slavery under dragons or wipe them out."

38

"Human-things?" Aurelle echoed.

"I'm not human," Nerra said. "The scale-sickness, the dragon-sickness... this is what it is. The potential for transformation. I told Greave that there was nothing to cure in me. I still think that. I am what I'm meant to be."

"You met Greave?" Aurelle asked, latching onto the part that mattered most. Hope rose in her that he might be nearby, and that she might soon be reunited with him. "He found you?"

Nerra hesitated for what seemed like a long time. "Aurelle, there's something I have to tell you."

Aurelle froze at those words, because they never preceded anything good. "What is it?" she demanded. "Is Greave okay?"

"Greave... my brother is dead," Nerra said, and only the pain in her voice stopped Aurelle from lashing out again at her.

"No," Aurelle said. "No, it can't be true."

"Shadr killed him," Nerra said. "I tried to stop her, but she slaughtered him like... like he was just an animal."

It was as if everything around Aurelle came to a halt in that moment. Nerra was still talking, trying to explain or telling her the details of what had happened, but Aurelle couldn't even hear the words. The pain of her grief in that moment was too great. It stopped her from thinking, stopped her from moving. She heard a wordless howl of pain, and dimly, Aurelle realized that it was her own. A part of her felt as if thinking that she'd lost Greave once before should have done something to lessen this, should have somehow prepared her, yet it hadn't come close. Instead, it felt as if Nerra had reached into her chest and ripped out her heart.

Nerra's arm went around her, and Aurelle shook her off, wheeling to face her, drawing a fresh blade from its hiding place.

"Don't try to comfort me!" Aurelle spat at Nerra. "You were there! You were a part of this!"

"Shadr did this," Nerra replied. "And afterwards... she wouldn't even let me grieve for him. Being connected to her meant that she filled my head until there wasn't any room for me left. It was only when I got away from her that I could even feel anything."

Aurelle let out another roar and threw herself at Nerra. Again, though, the former princess was too fast for her, and quickly twisted the knife out of her hand.

"Killing me won't do any good," Nerra said.

Nothing would. Nothing would make the world better when Greave wasn't in it. Last time, Aurelle had set her sights on killing the men responsible for his apparent death, but this time, how could she hope to kill a dragon?

"Do you think I don't feel it too?" Nerra asked. "Every step I've taken away from Shadr has let me feel more of the grief, more of the pain. My brother is gone. I've lost one of the only people who ever cared about me. He even..." She paused as she seemed to think of something. "We can't change what happened, we can't bring him back, but you can at least help to finish what he started."

She reached into her robes and took out a vial of liquid. Aurelle almost knocked it from her hands, simply out of the pain she felt then.

"Greave brought this to me," Nerra said. "He said it was a cure for the scale sickness."

"He... he made it?" Aurelle said. She hadn't known that he'd managed it. "Then why don't you drink it?"

"I am not something to be cured," Nerra replied. "I believe that, but I *also* believe that people should have a choice. This substance could help *all* of those with the scale-sickness. Let the House of Scholars see it, and they will be able to work it out."

"You hope," Aurelle said. Yet there *was* a kind of hope in it. It had the potential to change everything. She took the vial, staring at it. Greave had been through so much for this.

"Hope is all there is now," Nerra said. "I have seen Shadr's thoughts, and she is terrifying. Against something like that, what is there except hope?"

Aurelle didn't have an answer for that, at least not at first. "There's love," she said. "Greave loved you. He went through more than you can know to get it. I'll do this, but not for you. For him."

"And because of him, I will do what I can to stop what's coming," Nerra said.

"And *can* you stop it?" Aurelle asked.

The princess's silence gave her an answer. With Greave gone, though, Aurelle wasn't even sure that she cared.

CHAPTER EIGHT

Nicholas watched his prisoners as they made their way back toward Sandport, down through the lower dunes and patches of rocky ground that occasionally stuck up from the sand in spurs. They moved along in near silence, and Nicholas suspected that any snippets of quiet conversation were aimed at working out how to escape.

Most of his attention was on the princess who was their leader. Erin was so far from what he'd expected her to be. He'd expected some terrifying invader, determined to impose her values on the Southern Kingdom, paving the way for an army to sweep south and slaughter everyone who tried to stand in their way.

There were *some* things that seemed to fit with that: Erin seemed as furious and as dangerous as any foe he'd fought, and he could definitely see her wanting to slaughter anyone who tried to stand up and bring together the people of the kingdom. Yet he suspected that there was more to it than that; with the things she said, it was like she was genuinely afraid of a new Ravin rising, and being every bit as bad as the old one.

A part of Nicholas could understand that. *He* didn't want another Ravin to be in the world, either. Yet stability mattered; safety for his people mattered. Nicholas would do whatever he had to in order to keep those people safe, and whatever he thought of Erin, he still couldn't shake the feeling that a northern army might be coming south in the wake of her little scouting party.

Wait, what *did* he think of Erin?

"What do you plan to do with her?" Ankari asked, walking up beside him and echoing Nicholas's thoughts so clearly that for a moment it was easy to forget that she didn't have the magic she pretended to.

"I'm not sure," Nicholas admitted, and normally he didn't admit to uncertainty in public, because that wasn't what a strong leader did.

"Ferrent will say you should execute them all," Ankari said. "Sarit is already suggesting that you should stake them out in the desert as a warning."

Nicholas shrugged; the responses of his head of guards and the desert warrior were obvious enough. "What do *you* say?"

"I'm more interested in why you haven't already," Ankari said. "If this were some pretender to the throne, or some other assassin, you'd have cut their head from their body quick as you could."

"True," Nicholas said. He didn't say that half the time, he did that because it was the most merciful thing. Sandport could be a cruel place, and his father's torturers and poisoners tended to assume that those he threw into the cells were fair game. It was better to kill some foes cleanly.

"So why leave her alive?" Ankari asked. She smiled faintly. "Unless you *like* her?"

Nicholas stared at her. "For someone who pretends to be old, you can be quite childish about these things, Ankari."

"Oh, I suspect there's nothing childish about the things you think when you look her way," Ankari replied, her smile broadening. "Is that it? Keep the foreign princess in your tower, and do what you will with her?"

Nicholas's look turned hard. "You know I would never—"

"Oh, I know," Ankari said. "So you'll keep her there as... what? A hostage against the north's good intentions? And you'll treat her well, and hope that with time, she'll come around to the point where—"

"Ankari, you're going too far," Nicholas said. "Still, the idea of a hostage sounds good. If we can hold her and the others to make sure that Sandport stays safe, we can protect everyone."

"That's what you're taking from this?" Ankari demanded. She gestured in Erin's direction. "Look at her, Nicholas, and tell me what you feel."

"I don't feel *anything*," Nicholas lied, and she gave him the look she'd spent so long working on, the one that was meant to suggest that her mystical powers were showing her more.

Honestly, it was almost a relief when Sarit yelled out from the front of the convoy.

"Ambush!"

Figures came up out of the sand, well hidden, but not quite well enough to avoid the eyes of one of the desert people. The ones attacking now looked like a mixture of nomads and soldiers, tribal symbols scratched out to leave just the letter *I*, written in bloody red.

Inedrin's people. Nicholas briefly looked around for his rival, but there was no sign of him. Instead, there were just the men rising up to attack, and there were more of those than Nicholas liked, enough that even he wasn't certain that they'd get a victory from here. They charged forward, bellowing Inedrin's name as they came to try and murder him. Nicholas felt the familiar rush of excitement at the prospect of battle rising in him, along with fear for his people, and anger that Inedrin should have made it so far.

Nicholas drew his sword and his long knife, let out his own battle cry, and leapt to meet them.

*

The only other time Erin had seen Nicholas St. Geste fight, she'd been too busy trying to work out the best way to kill him to really appreciate it. Now, tied to the line of her friends, she watched him charge at the advancing line of those who had come to kill him, and there was something beautiful about it.

It wasn't that he moved like some delicate duelist from the House of Weapons, although there *was* a kind of grace to his movements as he swayed out of the way of one strike, then drove his sword through a man's ribs. Erin saw him block the stroke of an axe with the knife he held in his left hand, giving ground until one of his warriors could slam into the attacker from the side, the two going down in a tangle of violence. She saw him strike at another man, feinting high and then slipping under his attempt to parry, sword hacking into his ribs.

A part of Erin could have stood there and watched him all day, balanced between grace and violence, strength and agility. Yet in the moments that followed, there was so much violence around them that it was hard to keep track of any one combatant. Erin saw one of Nicholas's people go down with an arrow in his throat just a step or two away from her and the others, saw one of Inedrin's men pierced by a spear only to pull himself down it, stabbing at the wielder in turn. The violence around Erin kicked up dust and sand, until in just moments it was hard to see more than a little way in front of herself.

Her eyes fixed on the sword of a man who had fallen near her.

"This way," she called to the others, forcing Sarel and Yannis, Bertram, Ulf, and Nadir to shift over to the right with her, their bonds holding them to one another but still giving plenty of leeway for Erin to get to the weapon. It was a curved sword perhaps as long as an arming sword, but lighter, and obviously very sharp. When Erin set its edge to the ropes that held her, the strands parted easily. As her hands came free, Erin moved to first one then another of her crew, setting them loose in the midst of the battle.

"Get clear," Erin said to them. "Grab what you can and run. I'll try to meet you out in the desert. If I don't, try and make it back north."

"And what are *you* planning to do?" Sarel asked.

Erin stared out into the battle. "I'm... not sure yet. *Go.*"

She pushed them out into the battle, and they stumbled through the dust. Erin had no time to watch them, though, because she was already throwing herself into the fight.

She struck at those of Inedrin's men who came near. She had no illusions about them sparing her if she pointed out that she was Nicholas's prisoner, not his friend. A large man with a two-handed sword ran at Erin, and she barely dodged aside from it in time. Her opponent dodged back from the first of her return cuts, but the sword was light enough that Erin reversed the sweep and brought it back across her foe's throat.

She felt the thrill of the battle running through her, falling into the balanced space that Odd had spent so long trying to teach her. In it, Erin saw the next of her foes coming at her with a spear, and she seemed to have forever to brush the attack aside, grab the haft, and wrench the weapon from his hands. She slammed the butt of the weapon back into the man's face twice, hearing bone break as she did.

The spear was too long, so Erin cast it aside, keeping going with her stolen sword instead. She plunged forward, and now she was at the heart of a knot of Inedrin's men, cutting all around her, trying not to stay still for even a second. The dust that the battle kicked up helped, leveling the odds by letting Erin come out of nowhere to strike. Still, it got in her eyes and her nose as she fought, stinging as badly as the small wounds that seemed to appear as if by magic from enemy cuts. The ones Erin gave in return felled men, leaving them writhing in agony, or in the stillness of death.

She parried a jarring blow, cut a man's head from his shoulders, and now it seemed that Inedrin's men were turning to run around her. Erin whooped with a kind of feral delight, looking around for her next foe.

She saw Nicholas then, trading blows with a bulky swordsman who was clearly no match for his skill. She saw him twist aside from a thrust, just barely, and bring his sword down reversed, in a thrust that ran all the way through the man's chest, pinning him to the ground.

Erin saw a chance then, to finish this, to rid the world of another would-be Ravin. Even then, she hesitated, because after speaking to Nicholas, it seemed almost wrong to cut him down. It needed to be done though. It *had* to be done. She started forward, raising her stolen sword and bringing it down in a broad slash that would at least end this cleanly.

She must have made some sound though, or hesitated too long, because Nicholas was already turning, his sword rising to meet hers. They met in a resonating clash of metal that forced Erin to take a step back, and then they were facing off again, as they had before in the ruins.

There was no fight this time, though, because Nicholas's men were there then, several of them with bows leveled at her. His companion, Sarit, seemed to be raising a hand to give the order to shoot…

"Everyone stop!" Nicholas called out, and the power in his voice was enough that they all obeyed him instinctively. "This is done."

"Her friends are fled," Sarit said. "I will—"

"Leave them. Let them go," Nicholas said. "If the princess will disarm, let them go."

He held out a hand expectantly. Erin had a moment to think about it, but she knew she didn't really have a choice. She'd blown her best shot to kill him. Sighing, she threw her sword down in the dirt at Nicholas's feet.

"So what now?" Erin demanded. "Are you going to kill me?"

"She tried to cut you down," Sarit said.

The woman who played at being a seer, Ankari, stepped close. There was blood on her outfit now. "I saw her cut down plenty of Inedrin's men, too. And she has value as a hostage."

"None of that matters," Nicholas said. He stepped closer, and there was a hard look in his eyes that Erin guessed might have made most people fear for their lives. Erin met that look head on instead.

"Aren't you afraid of me?" Nicholas asked.

"No," Erin shot back.

"Good." He took her hands and tied them again. "Thank you for helping in the fight. Don't try to escape again."

That was it? He wasn't going to say more than that? Erin found herself almost disappointed, and not understanding *why* she was disappointed. Simultaneously, she found herself wishing that she'd cut him down, and strangely grateful that she hadn't. It made no sense. She couldn't even work out why he'd let her live, after she'd tried to kill him.

Still, it seemed that she would have all of the journey back to Sandport as his prisoner in which to work it out.

CHAPTER NINE

Shadr could not feel the princess she had chosen as her own. She flew high above Astare, but there was no sign of her, landed on its highest tower and called for her, but she did not come. Where before, Shadr had been able to feel Nerra's thoughts as a small fragment nestled among the great bulk of her power, now, she was absent, gone... she had left Shadr behind.

Anger flared in Shadr at that, and she blew a burst of shadows out into the sky, blotting out the brightness of the sun for a moment or two. A part of her longed to go and hunt down the Perfected she had taken as her own, to find her and bring her to heel the way a human-thing might train a reluctant hound. There was too much in play right now for that, though.

Shadr could feel the force of dragons she had sent south to strike at the city, *their* thoughts never truly likely to fade away from the great web of connections that constituted her mind. One of the Perfected might come and go from that connection, but other dragons were always a part of it. To be one dragon was to be all dragons.

Even so, they grew more distant, their hunger and their joy in the air less than that of the creatures around Shadr, the mission Shadr had given them less of an overwhelming command in their minds. Shadr coiled around herself atop her tower, waiting, her frustration at not being able to act hard to contain.

Her frustration only grew as she felt the rumblings of discontent rising among some of the others there. Letting her attention fall into the space that dragons shared between them gave her their words, and their disloyalty.

She has led us poorly, one sent, the feel of its mind like old paper against Shadr's. *Our queen has led us here, and bade us to slay, yet now we sit like basking lizards, doing nothing but hunt sheep and fish.*

Few enough of those, another replied. To Shadr, its consciousness felt wet, cool with the depths of the ocean. She knew it would be one of the dragon kin who swam as much as flew. *The fish flee to other grounds, and kept here, I cannot follow.*

47

Shadr reared up on her tower, stretching, but not wanting to act yet. She wanted to hear all that those around her had to say. She wanted to understand the depths of their discontent.

She leads us to disaster, one with a mind like hot sand whispered. *The amulet bearer lives, and yet she has sent a flight of our brethren against them.*

Another's agreement was easy to feel. *All after she promised that she would deal with that one, draw him out and kill him. What has she achieved, except to lose her Perfected?*

Now Shadr could stand it no longer. She drew herself up and spread her wings, opening her mouth wide until she could blast forth flame in a torrent above them all, the noise of it against the air enough to draw their attention. She roared then, deep and low, reminding them of her power.

Do you forget that I am your queen? she demanded, her thoughts echoing out among them, strong as a blow. *Do you forget that I lead you to vengeance against the human-things for all they have done? They controlled us. They destroyed our eggs!*

The force of her mental shout was such that some of the Perfected below reeled from it. Shadr didn't care. Let them all hear. Let them remember her power. In the silence that followed, though, another voice spoke up.

There were other times, after, it said. *There were times of peace with the human-things, not as rulers, but as equals.*

They are not *our equals!* Shadr replied. *They are foolish, mammalian things, no more than food that can talk!*

For a moment, she thought that she had quelled them, but then the voice started again.

Your memories might not run so far. The queen who was your ancestor died before that time, it said. *But I remember peace, I remember kindness and friendship.*

Shadr roared back her rage. *I remember their swords. I remember them slaughtering my kin, my brood...*

That was not you, but your ancestor, the other dragon insisted. Shadr found the one that was speaking now. It was a pale golden thing, almost as large as her, with fronts of scales around its features like a lion's mane.

Shadr leapt at it, taking to the air and diving at it without warning. She blasted it with shadow as she leapt, the power of it striking the golden dragon even as it tried to rise into the air to defend itself. Shadr felt the shock around her from the other dragons.

No challenge. There was no challenge made!

Shadr didn't care. The other dragon managed to rise into the air, but it was injured now, wheeling around only slowly to face her. It managed to avoid Shadr's next strike, though, rising higher into clear air.

This is what happens to those who will not obey! she sent out, blasting out another gout of shadow toward the golden dragon. It met that shadow with flames, the two cancelling one another out, but that gave Shadr a moment to climb still further.

In the air, everything was a battle for position. Animals, human-things, thought in two dimensions. A dragon had the whole sky in which to fight, so that everything was about who could get behind whom, who could get higher, or all the way under where the belly was softest. Shadr had risen this time to a spot where the sun was directly behind her, making it hard for the golden traitor to judge how fast she was coming, or what she would do as she struck.

Of course, her golden foe tried a lance of flame aimed at her as she dove. Shadr had been expecting that, though. She rolled aside from it in midair, carried on through, and struck her opponent with the force of a falling mountain. They tumbled together, clawing and biting, wings barely slowing them, but Shadr made sure that she stayed on top as they fell.

She felt a claw rake her side, felt teeth pull at her scales. It didn't matter. All that mattered was height, and what could be done with it. They kept plummeting, and now they struck the roof of a spire, point so elongated that it was like a spear. Shadr drove that spear deep into her foe's back, driving the golden dragon down onto it to impale it. The dragon hung there, trapped, limbs flailing as it tried to get free.

You have won, a dragon called. *Victory to the dragon queen.*

Shadr ignored it, flying around the golden traitor, observing it with cold eyes.

I yield, O queen, it tried, even the voice of its thoughts feeble.

Traitors don't get to yield, Shadr replied, and ripped its throat out with her teeth. The blood was warm, the golden dragon's last shriek of rage and pain turned into a bubbling mess by her teeth. She tore at it the way one of the Lesser might have at an animal, wanting to make her point, wanting to utterly destroy this foe.

49

She rose, her maw still bloody with the meat of her foe, and settled in place on the tower she had taken for her own.

I am your queen! she sent out to the dragons around her, accompanied by a roar of triumph.

A queen who does not honor the challenge. A queen who kills other dragons.

Shadr whipped round, trying to find the one who had sent out that thought. She would slay it like the golden one.

How many will you kill? another asked. *We are your kin, but you treat us like the Lesser, there only to obey or die.*

Shadr snarled at that, breathing out a burst of shadows.

None shall question me.

That just earned her another comment from the edges of thought, impossible to pin down.

A leader who wants us to kill the humans must be questioned.

Shadr sent out another blast of shadow, scraping it along the sides of one of the black stone buildings there.

None shall speak of the human-things as anything other than creatures to be slaughtered!

She stood there, waiting for them to roar back their approval, to get caught up in the blood lust she pulsed out at them. Instead, Shadr found a single word echoing around the minds of those there.

Tyrant.

The word seemed to bounce around Astare. Not all of them were thinking it, but too many were. Too many to hope to slay for their disloyalty.

Tyrant.

Shadr roared at those who dared to voice such a thing, but they didn't even try to fight her. Instead, they turned their backs on her, spinning on their perches like she was nothing, as if she didn't even merit their attention.

Slowly, one by one, they started to take to the air.

Stop them! Shadr called out to the ones who remained. *Slay the traitors!*

They made no move to do it, though. Perhaps they were afraid that there were too many of them to fight like that, even if most still stayed there. Perhaps they had the same objections to slaying other dragons that the others had voiced, in spite of being willing to stay. Perhaps they just saw that once such a fight started, it would not stop.

The traitors took to the air one by one, some swooping low to pick up Perfected as they went. Shadr saw the flash of blue scales among them as Alith, the dragon Nerra had first bonded with, flew among them. She had no doubt that it had played some part in this. The flight of dragons flew slowly, heading west, and Shadr had no doubt that she could catch them if she tried, but what then?

Let them go, she thought at the others, as if she had any choice in it. *The traitors deserve one another.*

She flew down at the perch one of the traitors had chosen, a blocky house of black stone. Her claws raked it, her tail whipped round to batter it, smashing stones apart from one another. Destroying it didn't even begin to vent the rage she felt at not being able to control this, at her kind just *ignoring* her. Shadr spat flames and shadows into the sky, roaring her frustration and smashing another stone building. Only when the first rush of that rage was spent did she fly back up to her tower, settling into place there, looking around at the rest of them in challenge.

The ones who left are weak, she told them. *We are strong. We will not seek peace with the human-things. We will destroy them!*

She roared it and spread her wings, her anger still racing through her. There was so much anger, had been all her life. From the moment Shadr had hatched, she had known the anger that came from memories of the old queens. She had felt every cruel thing their human servants had done when they had betrayed their dragon rulers. It was time for them to pay for that.

Their cities will become dust, she promised. *Their homes shall know flames, and the powerful among them will learn that they are no more than food.*

Now, the others roared their support, because the ones left were the ones who loved her for her power, or agreed with her, or both. Shadr reveled in it, bathing in the wash of approval the way she might have basked in the sun.

She was so busy doing it that she almost didn't notice the human-thing who approached onto her tower, having somehow gotten through all the dragons of the surrounding city.

CHAPTER TEN

When Anders first saw Astare, he'd marveled at the destruction the dragons had wrought in its outer city. Now, he was grateful for it, because the rubble and the blackened ruins of houses were the only things providing cover to let him get closer.

This was what he'd been born for, a moment like this. Him, not Devin. *He* was the one approaching an army of dragons, about to use the amulet that could change the tide of any conflict with them. *He* was the one whose name would go down in the annals of history for today. The man who controlled the dragons.

First, though, Anders had to reach the dragon who mattered: the queen. That meant slipping into the very heart of the city, when there were hordes of lizard-like things around it, and dragons perching on every rooftop of the inner city.

He abandoned his horse well outside the limits of the city. There was simply no way it would approach closer with so many powerful predators there. Maybe if what he had to do hadn't been so close at hand, Anders wouldn't have approached closer either.

How to sneak past an army of beasts, when one might be a challenge for a strong man to fight? Magic held part of the answer, in a spell to mask Anders's scent, twisting the air around him away from the noses of the creatures. Disguise was another part of it, since some of the creatures, the ones that seemed to speak and reason rather than simply raging, wore cloaks and robes, tunics and other articles of clothing that only barely changed their strange nature. It helped, too, that there seemed to be no humans left in the city, those there having fled or been killed. Why would the lizard creatures look for a human when they knew there were none to find?

Even so, Anders relied on stealth to keep himself alive. He kept as low as he could as he approached the outer city. When he'd been a boy, his tutors had crept up on him through fields and orchards, city streets and mazes of rooms. They had fired balls of stinging pepper at him when they spotted him. At the time, it had seemed like one more small cruelty in the name of making him the one he was meant to be. Now, he was grateful for it.

Anders moved from cover to cover, slipping behind the destroyed frame of a cart, then the half-fallen walls of a shack. He moved without a sound, judging with every step where he would be visible from, where the light fell and the shadows, which walls and fences, fallen beams and piles of bones would break the lines of any watchers' sight. Anders judged every move he made, thinking through not just the one ahead, but the ones after that, and after that too.

To some extent, the very chaos of the creatures around Anders made his task easier. They fought among themselves, and in some cases fell on one another to devour the weakest among them. Anders saw *some* food there among them: sheep and cow carcasses, even the remains of some of the former inhabitants, but there probably wasn't enough for all of them. They were hungry, and that hunger was fueling their chaos.

Anders could pick out patterns in the way the moved, similar to the way schools of fish might move in the ocean. Anders tried to time those movements, continuing into the gaps, staying out of sight. He got closer and closer to the gateway to the inner city, which still stood in dark stone, providing the perches for the dragons.

There was a simple problem there, though, because a large group of the more bestial creatures stood in front of the open gates, and Anders couldn't see a way through. He could try to climb the walls, but that would leave himself too exposed for too long. Anders had no wish to be plucked from them by some sharp-eyed dragon.

He considered the problem for several seconds before he came up with a grim solution. It was dangerous, but he suspected it would work, so he waited until the wind was in the right direction and let the spell that masked his scent fall for just a moment. Instantly, Anders saw the creatures react, their snouts sniffing the air. They started toward him, and Anders put his spell back in place, slipping back through the cover he'd found, climbing up onto the second floor of an otherwise fallen house and waiting.

The creatures reached the spot where Anders had been, then sniffed in obvious confusion, clearly not understanding why his scent had disappeared again. They spread out, obviously searching for him, and Anders waited in silence, his sword drawn. He waited, letting them spread out, knowing that if he timed this wrong, he would be facing a whole horde of them at once. They spread, searching for him, sniffing for him, until one was left below him, trying to find him.

Now.

Anders dropped, leading with the point of his blade. The creature looked up as he fell on it, but as dangerous as it looked, it had no time to react to him. The sword pierced its skull, and Anders felt the impact as he crashed into it. The fall threatened to knock the air out of him, but he knew there was no time to waste. He forced himself back to his feet and quickly hacked the creature apart, leaving it as he headed closer to the gate.

Then, it was just a question of waiting until the scent of blood and meat drew the lizard creatures to it, giving him a clear run through the gate into the old city. Anders sprinted through, and immediately flung himself into the cover of a building.

Dragons sat above, so many that it seemed impossible. Anders would have stared at them in awe, except that they presented a problem. Each was an aerial predator, and Anders had no doubt that they would have sharp senses to pick out prey on the ground. His cloak and his stealth would help him a lot as he made his way through the city, but Anders suspected that there was simply too much open ground between him and the tower on which the great black dragon sat to make it without being seen.

He waited, trying to plot a route through the inner city that wouldn't get him killed. There seemed to be no way of doing it, though, not without a distraction. Somehow, Anders suspected that the trick he'd used with the smaller beasts wouldn't work with these much larger foes. Anders could feel the amulet pulsing against his flesh, seemingly responding to the presence of so many dragons, but he couldn't get close to the one he wanted to use its power on the most.

Then, without warning, Anders saw the great black one on the tallest tower fling itself into the air, striking at a golden dragon, the two engaging in brief and bloody conflict. Anders found himself staring at that fight, and realized that all the other dragons were staring too. He had his chance.

He ran for the tower the black dragon had perched on, reasoning that it would return to the same spot. Fragments of black stone as big as Anders's head fell around him as the creatures struck buildings, and a glance up showed him the moment when the dragon queen impaled her rival on a spire. Anders couldn't stand there watching what followed, though, because he still had ground to cover before he made it to safety.

He plunged into the tower, finding it largely empty, the contents ripped apart by claws. Once inside it, Anders dared to breathe a sigh of relief, but he couldn't stop; the pulsing of the amulet was too insistent for that by now. He looked around until he found a stone staircase winding its way up through the interior of the tower, and started to climb.

There was wreckage on each floor of the tower. Judging by the little that remained, this place had once belonged to a member of the House of Scholars. Perhaps there were still secrets to be found here, yet Anders found that he had no interest in looking for them. Anything he might find seemed paltry in comparison to the power that roosted just above him.

He looked out the windows of the tower and saw some of the dragons take flight. Were they all leaving? Was he about to climb all this way for nothing? No, he couldn't allow that. He redoubled his steps.

Finally, Anders saw open air above through a hatch. He climbed through it, and found himself on the roof of the tower, along with the great bulk of the largest of the dragons. This close, it was magnificent, powerful in a way he hadn't believed a dragon could be. It made the ancient one they had found in the volcano look small by comparison.

Its head came around, staring at him with huge, snakelike eyes, and Anders realized that he'd been staring too long. He grabbed for the amulet he wore, knowing as he did so that if this didn't work, he was about to die. The dragon opened its mouth, and Anders was sure that he saw the first sparks of flame beginning there.

Then he touched the amulet, and the magic flickered into being.

"Obey me," Anders told it, told *her*, because now Anders knew this dragon, could feel its mind as surely as his own flesh.

Obey you? the dragon replied. *I am Shadr, queen of dragons. I obey* none!

The dragon started to rear over him, and Anders felt fear in that moment because he was sure he had miscalculated. He'd assumed that the amulet would make this easy. Now… now the dragon's jaws were opening to devour him.

"No," Anders said. He poured his will into the amulet.

He felt the dragon's will like a mass in front of him that his power pressed against, too huge to even begin to move. Even so, Anders threw his will at it, and his magic, focusing it through the amulet, hoping that it would be enough as he saw flames start to gather in Shadr's mouth, her power forming to blast him out of existence.

He felt the vast edifice of her will start to shift.

"Obey me!" Anders roared at her. He threw everything he had at her, knowing that if he held back even a little, he was dead. He felt the moment when something shifted, the amulet connecting to her, its power forging a chain of magic that ran between them in a single shining thread.

Yes, Shadr replied, as the magic compelled her.

Anders felt that connection, but more than that, he felt it spread. He felt Shadr's power as the queen of the dragons, felt her place at the heart of a web of connected minds, felt the dragons as thinking, powerful beings. Then the power of the amulet started to wash through that connection, joining the minds there to his service like a king taking fealty from his lords and their knights in turn.

He felt the power there in Shadr, and in the dragons who followed her. This was a creature who used magic as easily as breathing it out as flame or shadow, who could fly to the furthest corners of the kingdom, and beyond. Anders realized then just how small he'd been thinking in believing that he could return to Royalsport and just be a hero. He could rule there if he wished, and not just there. He could take the Southern Kingdom too. He could go to Sarras, and unify all of it. With the power of the amulet and that of the dragon queen thrumming through him, anything seemed possible.

He could feel something else, too: Shadr's hatred at being compelled, her desire to end Anders and all like him. To Anders, though, that was simply proof of why this was necessary. Creatures like this had to be controlled by someone like him, or the world would fall into terror.

"Lower your head," Anders told Shadr, and the dragon queen did it as gracefully as a swan bending its neck.

Anders climbed atop her, gripping her scales, feeling the strength of the creature beneath him.

"We will show the world what I have saved it from today," Anders said. "We will go to Royalsport, and they will yield power to me. I will take their queen as my wife, and rule as the savior of the kingdom."

56

And if they will not yield? Shadr's voice had a whispering quality to it, something filled with power, but with an edge of subtlety to it. Anders could feel that she was trying to manipulate him, but it made no difference.

"Then I will simply *take* the kingdom," Anders said. "Fly, my dragon."

He felt the surge of energy as Shadr took to the air, powerful wings propelling her. Around her, the other dragons there launched into flight in a deadly flock that might destroy the world if Anders chose. It was an awe-inspiring power…

…and it belonged to Anders, to do with as he wished.

CHAPTER ELEVEN

Nerra was wandering blindly when she saw the dragons. She had nowhere to go now that she'd fled Shadr, so her only thought was to put distance between herself and Astare, crossing farmland, heading south.

The presence of dragons flying in formation told her how futile that hope was. They were moving quicker than she ever could, wings eating up the leagues faster than even her Perfected body could carry her.

Instantly, Nerra sought a hiding place, crouching low and trying to shelter in the shadow of a solitary tree that stuck up from the farmland like a finger. She peered out from it, certain that this would be Shadr and the others seeking her out, determined to bring her back. Worse, maybe it was the armies of the dragons spreading out into the kingdom, determined to raze everything to the ground the way...

...the way she had helped to. Guilt filled Nerra at that thought. It was easy to blame the destruction on Shadr, but she'd played her part in it, and some of the destruction that they'd wrought together was down to her anger as much as the dragon's. She knew that she couldn't let Shadr find her again, because if that happened, Nerra doubted that she would have any will left with which to fight against the destruction the dragon wanted.

She couldn't see Shadr's great, shadow black form among the dragons there, though. Nerra stared out, trying to work out what was going on, and that was when she saw dragon eyes looking down at her. They'd spotted her.

Nerra ran. She fled with all the speed that her Perfected form granted to her, the countryside blurring around her as she did so. She leapt over a stone wall, thundered down a trackway meant for carts. She didn't look back, and didn't slow, knowing that any second, she might feel the sudden heat of dragon's breath on her skin, or might feel the piercing pain of claws impaling her flesh. Nerra didn't know what dragons did to Perfected who betrayed them, but that was only because, as far as she knew, none ever had.

She ran for all she was worth, and it still wasn't fast enough. The bulk of a dragon flew past Nerra, dust rising as its wings spread to slow its landing to something safe. It turned, and Nerra braced herself for death, knowing that there was nothing more she could do to protect herself, and that there was no way to avoid the heat or the pain to come.

It was only then that she took in the shimmering blue of the dragon in front of her, picking out the multicolored iridescence that ran through that blue. She *knew* this dragon, knew it as well as she knew any other dragon except Shadr.

"Alith?" Nerra said. She stepped forward hesitantly, holding out a hand. Had Shadr sent the dragon she had first connected with to hunt her down as some kind of test of loyalty? Had she been the one to find Nerra because of their connection? Slowly, carefully, Nerra put a hand on the dragon's flank.

Do not fear me, Alith whispered in her mind. *I will not hurt you.*

"But Shadr—" Nerra began.

The queen is a false one, consumed by hate, Alith replied. *Those with me see that. They seek a better way, but I cannot show them one without your help.*

"Help?" Nerra said, not understanding. "What do you mean? What's going on, Alith?"

Join with me, Alith sent to her. *Join to me as you did to Shadr, and you will understand. Do you allow it, Nerra? Will we be one?*

"Will you overwhelm my thoughts like her?" Nerra asked. "I couldn't even grieve for my brother. I did things, and I don't even know if it was *me* doing them, or just what she wanted."

It will not be like that with us. Shadr seeks to dominate. I seek... more than that.

"How much more?" Nerra asked.

Join with me and know, Alith replied.

Nerra tried to think. Did she want this? Did she want to be joined to another dragon? Did she want to give up her newfound solitude so easily? Except, she didn't have anywhere to go, anywhere that would accept her.

Please, Alith sent. *I need your help if we are going to stop Shadr from destroying the humans.*

That was enough to persuade Nerra. She'd lost almost her entire family. Her sister was left, back in Royalsport, and Nerra wasn't going to lose her too.

59

"Yes," Nerra said.

Alith raised a claw, striking at the small scales of one leg, scraping them from her. Nerra lifted one, knowing what to do. She pressed it to her heart.

She gasped as the scale sank into her flesh, becoming one with her through magic almost as old as the dragons themselves. She felt the connection between her and Alith blossom in that moment, and felt herself connected to the greater consciousness of all dragons. Through it, Nerra saw what she could only assume was the past, only this wasn't the past Shadr had shown her. It didn't feature humans bowing down to dragons, or trying to slay them in the night. Instead, they seemed to be working together, living in peace.

This is what came beyond the killing, Alith explained to Nerra. *A time when our kin and humans were able to coexist, and the world was a better place for it. It is a time Shadr cannot accept. She will rule humans, or she will destroy them.*

"But you don't feel that way?" Nerra asked. She looked around at the other dragons that still wheeled above them. "They all don't feel that way?"

We kill your kind, and they kill us, back and forth, until none are left, Alith replied. *When we retreated from human lands, and human memories, it was so that old wounds could heal, not so that we could gather our strength for the fight. With the magus who forged peace dead, we saw that there might be another war, so we took Sarras for our own, and retreated to its high places.*

Nerra had never expected to hear Alith like this, or to feel her emotions quite so close. She was used to the anger and casual dominance that came from Shadr, not to this other, more peaceful mind. She hadn't known that dragons could be like this.

Everything you know of us was filtered through her, Alith sent. *And everything we were was determined by our queen.*

"But you've broken away from her?" Nerra said. "You're rebels?"

A queen is not an absolute thing, Alith said. *If the queen who is your kin asked too much of her people, what would happen?*

"They would disobey," Nerra said.

And if she killed them for it? If she slaughtered them for even questioning?

"They would rebel," Nerra said.

60

Shadr slew one of us outside of the challenge. She did it simply because it questioned. So we rebel. We seek a better way. But first, we must stop Shadr.

"So we have to go back to Astare?" Nerra asked.

Not to the city of black stone, Alith replied. *Shadr is ready to fly south. She has already sent dragons ahead.*

To Royalsport, to kill and burn, to find the amulet bearer Nerra had guessed must be there.

"We have to stop them," Nerra said. "We have to stop them from destroying Royalsport."

We will fly fast, Alith assured her. *Ride upon my neck.*

She sank low for Nerra to mount her, and Nerra clambered up her scaled foreleg to settle into place on her back, clinging to her scales. It felt different to being atop Shadr. Alith was lighter and more graceful, smaller than the massive black dragon. That brought a thread of worry into Nerra's throat.

"Can you beat her?" Nerra asked. "If we have to fight, can you stop Shadr?"

I... do not know, the dragon answered. She glanced up. *But there are many of us, and this is a thing that must be done.*

She took to the air with Nerra clinging to her back. Nerra felt the powerful pulse of the dragon's wings, *her* dragon's wings. She felt it like something running through her own body. It felt so much closer than it had been with Shadr, as if this joining had always been meant to be. She lay one hand on Alith's back, the scales of her own skin the same brilliant blue as the dragon's. Here and there among the dragons who flew above, Nerra could see other Perfected clinging to those they rode. Did they feel this way, and if so, why had Nerra not felt this kind of pure joy of connection when it came to Shadr? Had the anger in the dragon just been too great for it?

How did they overcome hatred like that? As Alith rose through the air, Nerra counted the dragons around them. It was a good number, but not as many as those left behind, serving Shadr. Would they really be enough to save the humans of Royalsport? Did they have the strength to stop a dragon who was supposedly stronger than any of them?

Sometimes, Alith's voice whispered in her mind, *the only way to find out a thing is to do it. You saved me in the forest, little Nerra. You found my egg and saved me. Now let us save your people, and mine, together.*

61

CHAPTER TWELVE

Devin stood there in an open field with his hand on the ancient dragon's side, feeling its thoughts, understanding it in a way he'd never believed he would be able to understand something so utterly different from humanity. They'd taken a brief break from traveling after Anders, both so that he and Renard could rest a little, and so that the dragon could recover its strength after flying.

It also meant that Devin could explore more of the link that his magic seemed to have forged with this creature. He could feel the connection between them, the magic running like a thread between the two of them, yet Devin wanted to know more about it, wanted to learn more of this creature that had been old so many centuries before he'd been born.

The dragon seemed just as interested, observing Devin with great yellow eyes, its mind probing into him. The dragon's name, Memnir, rumbled through Devin's mind.

Once I was the companion of the greatest of magi, Memnir said, the words filled with a weight that seemed to come from age. *And now it seems that I am to be again. Hail to thee, Queen's Magus.*

"I'm not that," Devin said. "I'm barely much of an apprentice to Master Grey."

Forgive me. At my age, it becomes harder to focus on one moment in the path of time. You are *close to the queen of this land, though?*

"I'm not sure *what* I am to Lenore. The last I heard, she was holding some kind of dance to find a husband."

Just the thought of that tore Devin up inside. He'd thought, he'd *hoped*, that he meant more to Lenore than that. Now, he didn't know *what* to think, only that it hurt not being there with her.

"Ah, women," Renard said beside him. For his part, he was leaning against a tree stump, sharpening a sword. "Who can understand them? I thought things were fine with the lady of the House of Sighs, and then, inexplicably she's cold on me again. Of course, before that she wanted to kill me, so… oh, wait, you weren't talking to me, were you?"

"No," Devin admitted, keeping his hand on Memnir's flank. Curiosity got the better of him, though. "Exactly how many other members of the House of Sighs were you bedding at the time?"

"A few," Renard said, and paused in his sword sharpening. "What, you think *that's* why Meredith is wroth with me again?"

"Maybe," Devin suggested.

"But she's the head of the House of *Sighs*," Renard insisted. "Surely, if anyone would understand, it's her?"

Devin shrugged. "Maybe I'm wrong. The only person I've ever loved is Lenore."

"Love is a strange and wonderful thing," Renard said. "I could sing you many songs about it if you—"

"No," Devin said firmly.

No, Memnir agreed. Apparently the one Renard had used as a distraction had been enough.

"What I was *going* to say is that real life isn't like the songs," Renard said, standing. "Things are complicated. People love one another, but they have to do things because of the circumstances they find themselves in. Love itself doesn't solve anything; you still have to do... well, in your queen's case, all the things that are expected of a queen."

"That doesn't make it hurt less," Devin said.

"But it should give you some kind of hope," Renard insisted. "It means that Lenore might still care about you, and if circumstances become different... who knows?"

Devin wished that he could believe that. He wished that there were some hope for what might lie between him and Lenore. It was just hard to see how that might be the case when she would have picked someone to marry by now. No, it was better to focus on what they needed to do here.

"We should get going again," Devin said. "We still need to find Anders and stop him before he is able to use the amulet."

It would be quicker if I were to carry you, Memnir suggested.

"I don't know," Devin said. "I'll ask Renard."

"Ask me what?" the thief asked, instantly looking suspicious.

"Memnir thinks that we might catch up to Anders quicker if he carries us both," Devin suggested.

"Two things," Renard said, counting them off on his fingers. "First, the dragon has a name?"

63

"Yes," Devin replied. "I get the feeling they all do."

"But what kind of name is 'Memnir'?" Renard asked.

It is the memory that runs both ways, the touch of prophecy, the thought that lasts, Memnir explained in the privacy of Devin's mind. Devin knew better than to try to explain all that to Renard.

"And second?" he asked instead.

"No way, absolutely not," Renard said, sheathing his sword and folding his arms. "I've had enough of dragons to last a lifetime. There's no way I'm *riding* one into the bargain."

"It will be slower to walk," Devin pointed out.

"It's still worth it," Renard said.

Devin might have tried to argue with that, but there didn't seem to be much of a point. For now, it seemed that the two of them would be walking again, heading east and hoping that they found Anders.

They were about to set off again when Devin saw the first of the dragons in the distance. It shone the blue of the sky, light seeming to shine from it in bands of color that reminded Devin of a rainbow. Its wings beat slowly, the creature seeming to hang on the air, and it was only as it breathed flame ahead of itself that Devin realized that it was creating its own thermals on which to soar, rising up on their heat.

The young ones like to show off, Memnir mused, in a tone that clearly didn't approve.

Behind that first dragon, others followed, in a flight that Memnir seemed determined was not impressive, but which looked it and more to Devin. He had only ever seen one dragon at a time before, yet to see them in a great flock, soaring together, some with smaller figures on their back... it was impossible not to be awed by it.

Devin realized as he watched that the blue dragon had one of those smaller figures on its back too; it was simply that it was the same color as the creature's scales, so that it was hard to pick out one from the other. That dragon rider seemed to be pointing the way, directing the whole formation of the dragons.

Even as he stared at them, Devin tried to work out the direction of their flight. It took only a glance at the sun to work out that the dragons were flying south.

"They're heading for Royalsport," Devin said, watching as the dragons continued in their relentless course. The thought of what they might do there filled him with fear, but also determination to stop them.

"We don't know that for certain," Renard said.

64

"Where else could they be going?" Devin countered. "If the dragons want to take the kingdom, it makes sense to attack the one place left in it where a human authority is strong."

"And you think they're intelligent enough to think like that?" Renard asked.

"Yes." Devin nodded over to Memnir. "You said before that you'd held the amulet. You must have felt how intelligent they are."

"It doesn't work like that," Renard said. "The amulet creates a connection, but it's an artificial thing. Maybe a sorcerer could delve deeper with it and actually feel something, but for me, it was just a case of... well, mostly of holding it up between me and whatever dragon wanted to kill me at the time."

Devin guessed he could understand that. It was easy to forget, even for him, that not everyone understood the workings of magic. He was only just starting to understand the depth that magic had, and the need to balance the different forces of the universe exactly in order to apply power at just the right spot. Perhaps, then, it was obvious that a thief who had more or less stumbled into power wouldn't get it.

"They're as clever as you or me," Devin said. "Maybe cleverer. Their minds seem to touch one another, so that they talk, thought to thought. My guess is that their memories transfer across one to another as well."

They do, Memnir agreed. *It is necessary to allow our hatchlings to learn, when egg laying is so rare, and eggs are abandoned.*

Devin had a flickering understanding then of what it meant to grow up as a dragon. They were born alone more often than not, with no parent around to protect and feed them, because often that parent was dead. In a long-lived species, it was a way to ensure that their numbers did not grow too great, yet there was still something very lonely about it.

It also made the horde of dragons on the horizon even more impressive. They were solitary, intelligent creatures, banding together to strike out at humanity. Devin could imagine the damage that strike would do only too easily. If a force like that reached Royalsport, it might burn it to the ground without the people there able to protect themselves. The people there would die. *Lenore* would die.

"You're about to suggest something I'm going to hate, aren't you?" Renard said.

"We need to go after them," Devin said. "We need to find a way to stop them from destroying Royalsport."

Renard didn't look happy about that. "When Master Grey sent me up here, the idea was to find you and help save you if Anders had the amulet. He didn't say anything about going off after a horde of dragons when we don't even know if Anders is with them."

"If we don't, Royalsport might burn," Devin shot back. "And we have no way of knowing at this distance that Anders *isn't* with them. Sending a flight of dragons toward Royalsport seems like the kind of thing he might do."

Renard still didn't look convinced. "I've made a lot of foolish decisions in my life, Devin. Chasing after a bunch of dragons seems like it might be up there with the worst of them."

"You say you care about Lady Meredith of the House of Sighs? Well, if she's there, she'll burn with the city. Unless we find a way to stop those dragons."

"All right, all right," Renard said. "Do we at least have a plan for stopping them? Can you do with the others what you've done with this one?"

He does understand that I can hear him? Memnir rumbled in Devin's head. *This is the descendent of the old magus? This is one who bears his blood?*

"Memnir and I might be able to do something between us," Devin said, carefully ignoring that. "If Anders is there, we get the amulet away from him. If it's just dragons, then we try to convince them to stop. Memnir is old and powerful; they might listen to him even if I can't reach out with magic." He paused for a moment. "I'll understand if you don't want to come, Renard. You've done plenty just by getting me this far."

Devin saw the thief hesitate.

"That's not what I'm saying," he said. "I tried walking away already. I'm not going to do it this time. I just want to be certain that we haven't missed a way of doing this that *doesn't* send us hunting after a flock of dragons."

"If there is, I can't see it," Devin said. "Sorry." He looked at Memnir. "And I have worse news. While we were just tracking Anders, we could walk. Now, when we have to keep up with flying dragons..."

"You want me to ride on that thing, don't you?" Renard said.

Devin nodded. "Trust me, he's even less happy about it than you are."

He could feel the dragon's displeasure at having to carry the thief. Devin could only hope that Memnir wasn't planning to do anything about it. Devin had a connection with the dragon, but he didn't have the kind of control that the amulet supposedly gave. If Memnir decided to drop Renard in midair, there wasn't a lot Devin could do to stop him.

He only hoped that there was something he could do to stop the rest of the dragons, before it was too late.

CHAPTER THIRTEEN

"How is the progress with the weapons coming?" Lenore asked one of her scholars, as she and her retinue wound their way down a flight of stairs, into one of the castle's long halls. The man had to push his way past the others who followed her like the tail of a comet to speak.

The scholar was a middle-aged man who didn't wear their robes but who instead wore something closer to the practical workwear of a carpenter.

"The ballistae are progressing well, my queen," he said. "I have been collaborating with the House of Weapons, and they have been forging bolts with hardened tips that should be able to punch through scales."

Orianne walked beside Lenore, lowering her voice. "There is no word in the world more worrying than 'should' from a man who has only worked things out in theory."

Lenore turned to her as they passed through another doorway, into a small study. "And if I ask you how preparations are progressing to get people into the inner walls?"

"I would say that they *should* all be there in time," Orianne conceded, with a curtsey of apology. "And that we *should* have enough food for them all."

"We're working in a time of uncertainty," Lenore said, "but I don't like being uncertain about whether my people will be fed. Carry messages to the House of Merchants."

"And what should those messages say?" Orianne asked.

Lenore shook her head. "Honestly, I'm not sure it matters so long as you're the one to deliver them."

"Ah," Orianne said, "I understand. Let them see that their queen is watching what kind of efforts they make."

Lenore nodded. "Exactly."

Her maidservant hurried off to do it, and Lenore kept walking the castle, leading the way into an open space where a small, ornamental fountain stood open to the sky. Birds descended on it to drink. Lenore

68

found the sight soothing, at least until a dozen other people crammed into the space behind her. It also gave her an idea.

"Is there a scholar here who knows about the workings of the city's rivers?" she asked.

"One can be found, my queen," one of the scholars said. "What is it you require?"

"I want to know if the rivers of the city can be made to flood the city if needed to put out fires," Lenore said.

"To... *flood* the city?" the scholar asked.

"In a controlled way," Lenore said. "Find out, please."

He hurried off, going the same way as the others, and Lenore's procession around the castle continued. She led them through a series of receiving rooms, each one prepared by her ancestors to welcome different visitors. Some held masterpieces in silken tapestry work, although they were still bare compared to before the

"I also want the people organized," she said to one of the clerks who stood ready to take down her commands. "Send out criers to command that each household must have a man or woman ready to serve to help put out fires in their district, under the command of my officials."

There was so *much* of it to do, and at the same time so little that they could do. Lenore found herself wishing that her siblings were there, both those who were lost, and those who were out there in the world. Rodry would have been the first to try to stand against even a horde of dragons, and Erin wouldn't be far behind him. Maybe it was for the best that her sister was in the Southern Kingdom, put like that. Still, her presence would have helped to organize those troops that they had here. As it was, Lenore had sent to the House of Weapons for any remaining teachers who might be able to help formulate tactics for fighting dragons, and had sent messages to the nobles in the city asking the same, but she wasn't sure how much they could do.

Greave would have been just as useful. This was a situation that called for inventive planning, and he was good at that. No doubt he would have recalled some story from the history books about how people had fought dragons back in ancient times, and come up with some magnificent strategy involving throwing nets from rooftops to bring them to ground level, or running spiked wires between tall buildings.

69

Actually, neither of those sounded like a bad idea; Lenore resolved to add them to the list.

"Where is Master Grey?" Lenore asked.

"I believe he is still in his tower, my queen," one of her servants replied.

"Send another message to him. If anyone knows about defeating dragons, it will be him."

She didn't add that she wanted to hear if he had any news of Devin. It hadn't been long since he'd left, but it felt like forever with no news of the man she actually loved. She wished that he were there by her side, and she found herself reaching for the sword he'd made as a wedding present for her. Would this be sharp enough to cut through the hide of a dragon? Lenore sincerely hoped that she never found herself close enough to one to find out.

She led the way out onto the battlements of the castle, looking out over the city. It had been through so much in the last few months. It had been invaded, and then recaptured. It had been badly burned and partially rebuilt. The great buildings of the Houses still stood on their islands, but even they bore marks of all that had happened. The House of Weapons had considerable damage to it from the fighting, while the market around the blocky form of the House of Merchants was still depleted, and there were still too many people crowded around the House of Sighs, looking for shelter rather than there to enjoy its delights. The towers of the House of Scholars mostly stood untouched, but some had scorch marks from the attack of the first dragon. As for the city below...

It hurt Lenore to see some of it, but also made her proud. So much of her city had been burned or destroyed in the course of the invasion, either by the attackers or to try to stop them. Whole swaths of it had been damaged beyond repair, torn down or collapsed. Bridges had fallen. Now though, people were in the process of rebuilding. Lenore could see some of them below, working on their houses, or working to reinforce the bridges across the rivers crisscrossing the city.

How much more of the city would be destroyed in the face of a dragon attack? In that moment, Lenore could imagine it, the vast swaths of blackened buildings, the dead piling up in the streets. She could imagine the bridges fallen again, because creatures that could fly had no need of them, and the walls ruptured at their whim. Lenore had seen how much damage one dragon could do; could they even hope to stop an army of them?

In that moment, a part of Lenore longed to tell her people to flee into the countryside, to find safety anywhere they could and hope for the best. She knew that was the voice of cowardice, though. Her people would be no safer out in the countryside than they were here, and at least here they had a chance to fight back together, rather than being picked off as prey. Still, the pressure of knowing that many of them might be about to die weighed on Lenore.

She needed a break. It felt selfish, but *was* it selfish to want a moment of peace for herself, when that would leave her better able to do what was needed afterwards? She'd sent for Master Grey, but he could find her. Probably, he would be waiting for her when she went back to her rooms. Making a decision, she nodded to herself.

"That's enough for now," she said to the people following her. "You have enough to do for the time being. If you want me, I will be in my chambers, but I don't want to be disturbed for anything less than an emergency."

She headed back there, pacing through the corridors of the castle, heading up winding staircases, and along the passages that eventually led to her rooms. Lenore opened the double doors there, went inside, and then closed them behind herself, breathing a sigh of relief that she finally had a moment to herself.

These chambers were a sanctuary for her, opulent and gilded, yes, but also comfortable and safe in a way that so much of the castle didn't seem to be. At least, they weren't filled with people who wanted something from her, who needed her help to make decisions.

Yet there was one figure there, standing shadowed behind a drape. For a moment or two, Lenore thought that it *might* be Master Grey, there to help her, or to warn her about something relating to the dragons. Then the figure stepped forward, and Lenore saw him for who he was.

"Vars?"

Her brother looked... different, and not just because he was wearing rough sailor's clothes now. There was something that had hardened in him, as if whatever brief experiences he'd had in his time away had gone to the core of him. His skin was tanned and slightly weathered by life out in the open, his frame less soft around the edges.

"Lenore."

Lenore was shocked to see him here like this. She'd exiled him, told him that he had to leave her kingdom on pain of death. He shouldn't be here. It shouldn't be possible for him to be in the castle like this, having gotten past so many defenses and guards.

Yet he *was* here, and in spite of everything, Lenore was grateful for it. She was grateful that one of her siblings, even Vars, was here with her in the moment when everything seemed to be in so much danger.

She stepped forward and pulled him into a hug before he could stop her. She didn't care that he'd only ever thought of her as half his sister, or about all the things he'd done. If he was back here, then...

"What are you doing here, Vars?" she asked. "You know it isn't safe for you to be in the kingdom anymore. Why have you come back from exile? Did something happen?"

"I've come for you."

Vars stepped back from her, and Lenore's blood ran cold as she saw that there was something in his hand: a vial, the contents of which he poured into a scrap of cloth quickly and neatly.

"Vars?" Lenore said.

"The Hidden require your death," Vars said. He took another step toward her. "I'm sorry, Lenore."

Lenore tried to turn to run, tried to cry out for help from the castle's guards, but Vars was too quick for her. One arm wrapped around her waist, while the other brought the cloth up over her nose and mouth.

Lenore fought not to breathe. She fought with fists and feet too, trying to break free of the hold that Vars had on her. It made no difference, though, and the worst of it was that the exertion only hastened the moment when she had to take a gasping, choking breath. Whatever substance was on the cloth had a bitter tang to it, and almost as soon as she breathed it in, Lenore felt her body starting to go limp, strength leaching out of her.

As blackness claimed her the last thing Lenore saw was Vars's face staring down at her, no emotion visible on it.

CHAPTER FOURTEEN

There were dragons flying in from the north. Master Grey stood at the top of his tower and watched them with a mix of fear and determination. In that moment, Master Grey knew that they'd run out of time. Whatever preparations he'd made in his life, they had to be enough.

Master Grey had spent so much of his life preparing for this moment that it was hard to think of a time when he'd done anything else. He'd tried to postpone it and avoid it, tried to twist the balance of history away from it, and sought out prophecy in order to win through it. Now, here he was, in spite of it all, and the moment was upon them.

They came in a painter's palette of different colors, and each one seemed to have some slightly different grasp of the magic that powered their breath. Some spat mere gouts of flame ahead of them, but others managed to shape balls or ribbons of it, while still others seemed to belch clouds of gas or abrasive dust. Other creatures came below them, pouring forward in a horde of smaller figures that crept and ran, halfway between lizard and human.

They'd run out of time. Master Grey had hoped that by sending Devin and Anders out into the world, they might be able to stop this attack from happening, yet here it was. The moment that he'd been preparing for his whole life was upon them. It was time to alert the queen.

Master Grey hurried down through his tower, taking the steps at a speed that probably wasn't wise, given the length of his life. There was no time to waste, though, so he kept running, clutching his staff by his side as he sprinted for the great hall. Lenore would be in there, or if she wasn't, then it would be easy enough to send a servant to call her down to it. He ran in, barely slowing as the guards opened the doors before him, letting him into a space hung with banners and empty save for the throne at one end.

He skidded to a halt at the sight of the two figures who occupied the hall.

Verdant lounged, apparently without a care, on Lenore's throne. Vines wound around it, turning it into a throne of flowers, while her dress seemed to shift like a living thing on her skin. Her mask blossomed with the same blooms as the throne, and the madness in her eyes was obvious.

Void stood there beside her, pale mask utterly blank, robes pulled tight around him so that it was impossible to tell more about him. He stared at Master Grey in level challenge.

"Expecting someone else?" he asked.

"What are you doing here?" Master Grey asked. No, this couldn't be happening, not now. There was no time. The kingdom was in danger.

"Whatever we wish," Void said. "You interfered in our affairs, magus. You killed one of our number. We cannot let that pass."

"In any case," Verdant said, running a hand down the wood of the throne, so that flowers rose from it, "this is a very comfortable chair."

Master Grey wondered if their presence could be turned to his advantage then. "There are dragons approaching," he said. "Whatever you have planned, I will say this: help me to fight them, and you will be rewarded. We will not be enemies."

"A weak offer from a weak man," Void said. "You *offer* where we could *take*. You offer friendship when you have already wronged us."

"There is not time for this," Master Grey said. "Where is Lenore?"

"Oh, by now, she'll be dead," Verdant said. "Dead as a withered tree. Dead as bones buried beneath."

Anger rose in Grey at that. "Dead? You come here, *now*, and tell me that she's dead? With dragons advancing, you tell me that you've done this thing?"

"What's wrong, old man?" Verdant asked, dangling one leg over the side of the throne. "Things not working out the way you planned?"

Master Grey struck out at them then, throwing a pair of the glass orbs he'd prepared. He hoped to end this quickly, before either of them realized what was happening. If those orbs broke in front of them, probably even the Hidden wouldn't survive.

The orbs made it halfway before Void waved a hand and sent them spinning away to strike the far wall in a spray of force and fire. Instantly, he and Verdant struck back, Void flinging planes of raw force at Grey, Verdant causing vines to crack the floor near his feet, so that

74

he had to leap back to avoid them. A courtier looked in through one of the doors, and ran screaming.

The guards at the doors tried to intervene, rushing forward through the doors with swords already drawn. If he'd had any time, Master Grey might have tried to warn them, but as it was, he had to sink into the balance of his power, struggling to blow aside Void's attack with the all-too-still air of the room.

The guards died as they came forward. One tried to strike at Verdant, but she whispered a word and vines came up to wrap around him, crushing and strangling. The fate of the one who went at Void was worse. Void simply stared at him, and the man stopped, panting, and then screaming in what sounded like terror.

"No, no... it's... *no!*"

Grey saw him turn his sword upon himself, falling on it, because it was simply too much. Grey could do nothing to help either of them; he was too busy trying to summon his own power to fight.

He threw his staff and whispered a word. Runes on it flared, turning it into a spear as it went forward like a live thing, heading for Void's heart. The leader of the Hidden waved a hand, and now there was simply a gap in space into which the spear flew, disappearing completely.

Grey wasn't done yet, though. He pulled power from the air, setting it crackling with energy, so that merely to breathe it might be enough to kill. He found the force in the stones beneath the Hidden's feet that longed to break apart, and set it free so that they splintered into deadly shards. He kindled flames among their clothing, trying to turn them into human torches.

They countered each attack with ease. Void seemed to draw the crackling power from the air into himself, it simply disappearing deep into his being. Verdant conjured a carpet of grass over the stones, smothering them as Grey tried to break them apart. His flames briefly caught on Void's sleeve, but he sheared it off and sent it falling to the ground where it couldn't do any harm.

"All this time spent on subtlety," Void said, setting up moving planes of force around him that shifted and turned. "Carefully picking the point to apply power. Wrath could have set my whole being alight, yet you must focus on some tiny fragment of my sleeve to do *anything.*"

"Better that than selling half my soul to gain power," Grey said. He focused in on Void's workings, collapsing them in toward him, trying to kill him with his own magic.

Void waved a hand, and the workings disappeared. "You think that I have lost something, but it was nothing I needed. What has all your patient work gained you, old fool? You think that you have learned?"

"I have learned enough," Grey said. The last workings of a spell clicked into place in his mind, and he threw it at Void, the air itself tearing at him. Perhaps if it had just been him, it might even have worked, but Verdant was there, her plants moving to intercept the attack, shredding before it in Void's place.

"Let me show you what power is," Void said, and struck back with the kind of focused power Grey could only dream of. He parried the first blast of it, dove aside from the second, and felt searing pain as the third barely grazed his side. All three left holes in the floor as reality simply tore itself apart. In desperation, Grey reached out, calling to the stones of the ceiling and wall, using the touch of magic to tell them that they were lighter than they were, lighter than the air itself. They floated between him and the Hidden, and for a moment, that let him breathe. He *needed* to breathe, because the effort of something like this was immense.

Grey forced himself to one knee, realizing to his horror that he was losing this fight. He'd hoped that with one of them gone, and with him well rested, he might be able to take on the Hidden. Just two of them seemed to be too much for him, though. Even as he thought it, vines came up, wrapping his legs, holding him to the spot. He had to summon more strength than he'd hoped just to make them fall from him, withering and dying.

As he would die soon. Grey knew that there was no way out of this, which meant it was time to reach for the one spell that might end this, the spell he'd been starting to prepare the last time he'd fought the Hidden. He could unleash all the power that lay within him, let loose every scrap of balance, and the ensuing explosion would be more than enough to slay the Hidden. If he was to die, then at least he could rid the world of them.

"Oh, no you don't, old man," Void whispered.

Master Grey threw himself to the side as Void struck again, barely avoiding it, his concentration broken.

76

"Do you think we don't learn?" Void asked. "Do you think I don't know about your death spell? No, you'll simply die here, an unmourned old fool." He lashed out again, and this time Grey went spinning back across the Great Hall's floor, barely able to keep the spell from ripping him in half.

In that moment Grey understood the problem with his plan. The grim final casting took time. It took an effort of will to unbind everything in oneself, took careful casting, and the Hidden weren't going to give him a chance to do it. Already, they were pursuing him through the floating stones, and Grey knew that the moment they caught him, this time, he would die.

CHAPTER FIFTEEN

Somehow, Aurelle's second heartbreak managed to be worse than the first. She hadn't thought there was room for it, hadn't thought that anything *could* be worse than the sight of Greave lost in flames had been back at Astare. Now, it felt as if she'd learned one of the great truths about the world: things could always find a way to hurt more.

She rode her horse numbly back in the direction of Royalsport, but honestly, was there any point to it? She turned her horse slightly, riding in the direction of the coast road. A slope in front of her headed up, right to the edge of a cliff. Aurelle thought about simply heeling her horse forward and riding over it, but she knew that the animal would never do it. Besides, it deserved better.

She didn't. Everything that had been good in Aurelle had died with Greave. She'd turned away from serving Duke Viris because of him. She'd tried to do the right thing by asking herself what he would want her to do. Even her role in helping to put down the noble rebellion against the crown had come from seeking revenge for him. There was no revenge to take this time; at least, no revenge that Greave would want her to take.

There was only the chance to bring an end to all this. As Aurelle reached the top of the small rise, she dismounted her horse and looked out over the ocean. On another day, she might have thought that it was beautiful. Now, it just seemed bleak and empty, cold and deep. There were rocks below, at the base of the cliff, sometimes exposed, sometimes covered by the incoming waves. Aurelle didn't know if it would be better to smash on those rocks or to be swallowed by the sea.

She thought about leaving a note, but who would she write it to? Lenore? Meredith? The only person to whom she truly wanted to say anything was gone. She said it to the wind instead. Soon enough, that would carry her, so why not everything she felt?

"I loved you," Aurelle said. "I love you, and it feels like we... we never had a real chance. You were the only person who ever saw me as myself, even when I was lying about who I was. You made me want to be a better person. Now... now there's nothing. I can't do this again. I can't."

The words didn't seem like enough, but what words could ever *be* enough? What could express the depth of everything she'd felt and done when it came to Greave? She'd set out to fool him, fallen in love with him, lost him, killed for the memory of him. She'd traveled the length of the kingdom with him, and then back again. Now, there was nowhere left to go but down.

Aurelle stood there, poised on the edge, feeling the spray of the ocean on her face. She felt something else, too: the small weight of the vial that Nerra had given to her.

Aurelle took it out, examining it by the light of the sun. She was supposed to be delivering it to Royalsport, but right now, what did that matter? She went to throw it into the ocean, went to throw it away out of anger, and found that her hand wouldn't open.

She stared at it more, through what she realized was a haze of tears. This was the last thing Greave had worked on. It was what he'd gone with her to Astare to find the formula for. It was what had sent them both into danger, it was what had gotten him killed. She *should* want to destroy it, but then there would be nothing of Greave left in the world. He'd been incredible, intelligent, the kind of man who could have done great things, and this was the great thing he'd chosen to do.

If Aurelle threw it into the ocean, it would be destroying the work of the only person she'd ever truly loved. Lenore and the creature that was Nerra would remember Greave, but the act would take away the chance for Greave's work to change the world.

Aurelle took a step back as she realized that she couldn't do that. She couldn't take Greave's legacy from the world, and that meant... that meant she had to fulfill her promise to get it to Royalsport. However much it hurt, she had to do this.

"I'll finish this, for you," she whispered, as she remounted her horse.

Aurelle rode hard, heading south for the capital. The sooner she got there, the sooner the House of Scholars could start work on replicating what Greave had produced. Maybe if they did it quickly enough, there might even be a way for it to help with the fight to come. If there were more creatures like Nerra out there, maybe a trace of this smeared on a bolt or a dart might be enough to undo what had been done to them.

That was a thought for later, though. For now, there was only the need to ride hard, the wind whipping her hair behind her like the tail of a comet, the ground beneath her horse's hooves jolting with every stride. Aurelle pushed her horse now as hard as she dared, because she found that in the speed of the gallop, it was possible not to think about anything else for whole seconds at a time.

Still, she seemed to eat up ground far too slowly, the leagues falling away beneath her horse's hooves, but still more of them left. She passed over fields and forded streams, not stopping or slowing. The landscape was starting to become more familiar now, and soon, Aurelle was sure that Royalsport would come into sight.

It did, but so did the dragons closing in on it. They flew in toward the outskirts of the city, scaled and massive, multicolored and powerful. They breathed flames, and the grass of meadows beyond the city went up in walls of fire that surrounded the city as effectively as any army might have. Those walls of flame burned closer, leaving blackened ground behind them.

The dragons' creatures followed beneath them. Some seemed like Nerra had been, upright and wearing human clothes. More were closer to beasts than to anything human. They spread out, attacking anything they could find. Already, in the space beyond the outskirts, Aurelle could see a small hamlet aflame, could see people running, pursued by a trio of the more bestial creatures.

She *should* ignore them. She was no warrior, able to stand against her foes openly. There was nothing she could do there except get herself killed. Still, Aurelle found herself turning her horse toward the beasts following the fleeing people. On instinct, she took out the vial Nerra had given her, using the barest hint of the contents to coat the tip of a bolt designed for a hand crossbow. She charged into the fight in silence, because Aurelle knew better than anyone that a battle cry only gave enemies a warning. Even so, one was turning toward her by the time she caught up with them.

Aurelle trampled it with her horse, the creature going down in a crunch of bones as her steed impacted with it. She leapt clear, already flinging a knife to embed itself in the eye of another of them. The third had turned now, and was leaping at her, as fast and as strong as Nerra had been. Aurelle felt its claws scrape along her side.

However, while this one was faster and stronger than her, it didn't seem to have the same intelligence that lay within the more humanlike creatures. Aurelle feinted with one knife, then, as it was trying to follow the movement, stabbed it in the throat with another.

She struggled to her feet. Her side hurt, but there was no time to check how bad it was. The people who had been running were standing staring at her.

"Why are you standing there?" Aurelle demanded. "Run!"

They did as she commanded, and just in time, because Aurelle could see one of the dragons closing in then for another pass. If her emotions hadn't still been overwhelmed by Greave's death, she might have known terror then, because this creature was huge and red scaled, with claws that looked as if they could cut her in half. Instead, Aurelle found that there was no room for the terror amid the simple need to do what she'd promised herself she would. Dragons or no dragons, she would get Greave's cure to the city.

Aurelle ran for her horse, slapped it on the hind quarters, and set it running. She ran in the opposite direction, hoping that the distraction would buy her time to get clear. She took a zigzag path as she ran, and she was soon grateful for it as fire blasted down in a line, far too close to where she was. Aurelle had to throw herself to the side to be clear of it, and even so, the heat was so great that for a moment or two she was sure that it had struck her.

She *didn't* roll to her feet and keep running. That was the obvious move, and therefore the stupid one against an intelligent opponent. Instead, Aurelle hunkered down, letting the dragon think it had succeeded in incinerating her. She rolled into a patch of blackened grass that she hoped would not burn again, and waited for the dragon to pass.

Which would have worked, if there hadn't been more of the smaller creatures coming, apparently led by one of the ones like Nerra. Had the dragon sent them in to clean up after it and make sure no one survived? Aurelle hoped that it was just chance, but she knew that it didn't make a difference now. A few more seconds, and they would be close enough to smell her.

She took out a crossbow bolt and fitted it into a small crossbow. There was no way to take all of them, but maybe if she got the leader, it would be enough. Lifting it, Aurelle aimed for the creature's heart and fired. She cursed as she did it, because almost as soon as she shot, she realized that she hadn't allowed for the wind. The crossbow bolt flew out, but at the last minute curved slightly to the side, only catching her target a glancing blow, barely piercing its scales.

Aurelle knew then that she was dead. She shouldn't have stopped to help people, shouldn't have…

It was only then that she realized that the creature had stopped, falling to the ground, crying out in pain in an all too human voice. Its flesh twisted horrifically, and Aurelle felt like throwing up as she watched it. She realized in that moment that she'd used the crossbow bolt she'd dipped in Greave's cure, because what else could be doing this? She saw the creature throw up a clawed hand, and the others there turned, running in the opposite direction.

The hand didn't stay clawed. Instead, human fingers extended from it, and a human torso formed. Aurelle was left looking at a young man wearing the remains of simple gray clothes.

"Th…thank you," he managed to gasp, obviously still weak.

Aurelle wasn't looking at him though. Instead, she took out the vial of Greave's cure, thinking of how much he'd achieved, and how much she could do with that achievement right now. How much would the scholars need? Call it half, to be sure. How many bolts and daggers did that give her? She took them out, laying them out on the ground, trying to work it out. Would it be enough to get to the city through all this?

It would have to be. She wasn't about to let Greave down again.

CHAPTER SIXTEEN

Lenore woke slowly, and she was surprised to wake at all. She'd thought... she'd thought that Vars had killed her. She'd felt whatever poison he'd used on her seeping into her body, had felt the terror that she was about to die.

She didn't open her eyes for the moment, trying to learn all that she could from her other senses. She was lying on cold stone, and the air around her had a still feeling that might have come from being in a room that hadn't been opened in a long time. Her imagination automatically conjured some kind of dungeon, barred and mold filled. Lenore found herself thinking about the last time she'd been kidnapped, by Ravin's Quiet Men, and the terror she'd felt then of what might happen to her when they brought her to their king.

The fear now was a sharper kind of thing, because Vars had mentioned the Hidden before he'd drugged her. Lenore had heard stories about them, and the things they did. They were a nightmare made real, and if she was still alive, Lenore didn't want to think about the forces they might trade her to, or the experiments they might perform on her.

"I know you're awake." Vars' voice came from across the room. "I had to guess at the dose to knock you out for this. I suppose I misjudged it."

Lenore opened her eyes. To her surprise, she wasn't in a dungeon. Instead, she seemed to be in a tower room of the castle, one used for storage, judging by the boxes and trunks scattered around the place. The walls were bare, but they certainly weren't the dingy environment she'd been expecting.

Her brother stood there by the heavy oak of the door, stark shadows being thrown across his face by the light from one arrow slit window. It lent a dangerous look to his features, his expression impossible to read. Her crown dangled from one of his hands, the circlet looking unnatural there. Worse, the sword Devin had given Lenore sat at his side, fastened to his belt now.

"So is this where you kill me?" Lenore demanded. She looked around for anything she could use as a weapon. Vars wasn't coming toward her, though. "Why are you doing this?"

"I told you," Vars said. "The Hidden want you dead. You should stay here. Don't try to leave, if you know what's good for you."

Lenore wasn't sure what to make of any of it. The things Vars had said sounded like a threat, but he wasn't making any move to hurt her just yet. Instead, he was edging back toward the door.

"Stay here," Vars said again. "If you try to leave, things… things could get bad."

He slipped out of the door with that, shutting it behind him. Lenore stood up, trying to make sense of what was happening. Was Vars threatening her or not? It *sounded* like he was working with the Hidden out of stories to take her throne. That certainly made sense in terms of him drugging her and locking her away like this. Just because he hadn't been able to kill her, that didn't necessarily mean anything. Maybe Vars had simply not been able to do that final thing. Maybe he was planning on imprisoning her rather than killing her. Maybe he was saving her so that the Hidden could sacrifice her in some vile ceremony.

Which meant that, whatever Vars said, Lenore had to find a way out of there. She looked around quickly, and it was obvious that the window was too small to climb through, the walls solid, without any of the secret ways found in some other parts of the castle. She had no skill in picking locks, but even so, she tested the door, trying to see what she was working with.

She was quite surprised when it swung open.

Lenore couldn't imagine that Vars would have forgotten something so basic. Was this all part of his plan? Was it a trap? Lenore didn't know, and she hated not knowing. Maybe once, she would have been meek enough to just sit there, but not now.

She headed out through the door and down a winding staircase, down in the direction Vars must have gone, hurrying to try to catch up to him. She caught sight of him ahead and hung back, following without letting him know that she was there.

Was this some attempt to take back the throne? It seemed like a strange one, simply because Lenore wasn't dead. Vars knew what it took to take a throne, because he'd done it once. Yet he'd taken her

84

crown from her. This felt like something else, but Lenore wasn't sure what.

Where were the guards who should have stepped in to stop all this? Part of the answer was probably that they were engaged in the preparations Lenore had ordered, and that their numbers had been cut down by months of warfare anyway. Even so, Vars had managed to get her from her chambers to a tower room, and was now going down through the castle again, all without running into any of the guards who might have challenged him, or even cut him down.

She found an answer to that in the sight of one who lay dead, although clearly not from a blade. Vines covered him, strangling. A little way away, another lay comatose, simply staring into space. Something strange was going on here.

She kept following, and now she had to move from cover to cover to avoid the chance of being spotted. Lenore didn't know what Vars would do if he saw her; his threats had certainly sounded ominous enough. As they moved along a gallery, she ducked behind a plinth to make sure that he couldn't see her, then moved to press herself against a doorframe, watching him head toward another set of stairs.

Where *were* her guards? Vars was walking the halls of her castle with her crown dangling from his hand. Why weren't they stopping this?

It was only when she heard the roar from beyond the walls, and felt them shake with the impact of something huge, that Lenore understood. She crept over to a window and looked out over the city. What she saw there made her stop in horror; the dragons were there.

The outskirts of the city were already aflame, parts of them blackened by fire, parts flickering with orange and yellow sheets of it. Great columns of smoke billowed up into the sky, while Lenore realized that she could hear the screams of people below, running to get away from the attack.

The dragons soared above it all, wings barely beating, mouths open to pour forth flame. Some did it in wide arcs of fire, others in gulping blasts or precise lances of heat. It didn't matter; wherever the flames touched, Royalsport started to burn.

They weren't ready for this. That thought came to Lenore far too strongly. She'd done her best to prepare, sent her people out with orders to follow, ways to help the people of the city work together, but they weren't even *close* to being ready for this. Only a few of their

85

weapons were built, and her plans for a cunning system to flood the city to put out fires had come to nothing.

She could see some of her people below, trying to fight back, either against the dragons or simply against the flames. Chains of people with buckets threw water onto fires, only to scatter as the next dragon came over, breathing fiery death. The ballistae she'd ordered built tracked the dragons' movement and fired, one bolt tearing through a leathery wing. That just made this wave of dragons keep their distance from the main city, burning the outskirts without cease.

Below, the city was becoming a scene out of nightmares. There were creatures there that were human-sized but whose bodies had more to do with lizards than anything human. They roved the poorer city beyond the walls in packs, falling on those unlucky enough to get in their way. Lenore could see her soldiers on the walls, fending off more of them, killing them as they came forward in rolling waves.

For a few moments, Lenore stood there, trying to decide what to do next. A part of her told her that she should be out there with her people. She was their queen, and so she should go to them and try to organize the chaos below. Lenore could see the problems with that instantly, though: there was no controlling that chaos by running into it; people expected their orders from the castle. If she left it, and left Vars behind her here, then there would be no way to direct everything.

She had to deal with things here; she couldn't allow enemies within the castle as well as out there. Lenore would find out what was going on, and she would find a way to either stop it or use it for the defense of her city. Her mind made up, she went back to following Vars. She had to hurry to keep up, almost running after him as he rounded a corner.

She could see him now, and he seemed to be nervous, touching the hilt of the sword that now hung at his belt every so often as he walked. Lenore could hear him murmuring something as he went.

"I have to… I have to…"

Was he trying to talk himself into killing her? Lenore looked around herself, making sure that she would be able to find a hiding place if he turned around and headed back toward her. She didn't want to be caught out in the open.

For a while, it was hard to tell exactly where Vars was going. The castle was a big enough place, and it had enough twists and turns in it, that he could have been heading anywhere. Slowly, though, Lenore realized that he was heading for the throne room. He meant to do it, then; he meant to seat himself on the throne of the Northern Kingdom and set her crown upon his head. Even while dragons burned her city, Vars wanted to take it from her.

If Lenore had possessed a weapon, she might have used it on her brother then. As it was, she could only follow. Lenore found herself hoping for any ally who might help her in the fight against Vars, but it seemed that they were all either fled or helping in the fight against the dragons. Lenore would have to do this herself.

She followed Vars to the large, banded doors of the great hall. They hung open, revealing a scene of battle within that caught Lenore's breath in her throat. Master Grey stood there, behind a line of what seemed to be floating flagstones and fragments of wall, but only barely seemed to be standing. He seemed unsteady in a way that made Lenore frightened just to watch it.

Across from him, by her throne, were two masked, robed figures Lenore assumed had to be the Hidden. They struck out at Master Grey with things that seemed to be impossible: blades of pure force, thorny vines, bursts of gas coming up from flowers. They were using the kind of powers that Master Grey never seemed to show the world, and he barely seemed to be holding up under the onslaught.

Their eyes were fixed on him, so they didn't seem to notice when Vars stepped straight into the throne room, all but ignoring the queen's sorcerer. Not knowing what else to do, Lenore slipped in after him, hiding in a niche that held a suit of armor and a great shield with her family's coat of arms on it. There were ornamental weapons there, an axe and a sword. Could she find a way to do something with one of them that might help?

Lenore couldn't see an opening to do anything. Worse, it was obvious that Master Grey was weakening. One by one, the stones he had raised as a shield were starting to drop to the floor, each one striking it with the thud of stone on stone. Lenore had no doubt that when the last one fell, that would be the moment when her sorcerer died.

CHAPTER SEVENTEEN

Vars had to force himself to walk into the throne room, and his fears right then weren't just about being caught up in the enormity of the power being thrown back and forth in the fight between Master Grey and the Hidden. They were about everything he'd just done, and that he was about to do.

Once, he would probably have run from this. He still wanted to. All the way down through the castle, he'd wanted to run from the city, get out of there, and head back into whatever form of exile he could find. One glance out of the window had told him the dangers of that, though. How was he supposed to escape a city in the midst of a dragon attack?

Besides, he had to do this. If he ran, he had no doubt that the Hidden would find him if they lived, wherever he escaped to. There was no running from this, not when Lenore was left there behind him in the tower. He had to do this. Step by step, he walked up to the dais from which the Hidden were throwing their attacks.

Void threw a burst of power in Master Grey's direction, and Vars saw one of the last remaining stones he was using as a shield move into the way. The attack struck it and shattered it, sending a spray of stone fragments out into the room beyond. The sound of the impact was enough to drown out even the sounds of the battle outside.

Vars felt a fresh thrill of fear at that display of power. Even though the Hidden had brought him from one place with their magic, even though he'd seen Verdant change her appearance and seen flowers grow from nowhere, it was impossible not to be awed by the sight of someone shattering stone with no more than a wave of his hand.

Vars stood there by the side of the dais, and for several seconds, the Hidden's attention wasn't on him. They ignored him as surely as they might a servant, or a tool to be used. That brought a kind of anger up in Vars, but this wasn't about his anger.

Or was it? Maybe the difference in life was simply *what* some people got angry about. Rodry used to get angry about Vars's cowardice, or about the ways he failed to live up to the ideal of a knight. If she'd been here, Erin would have been angry about all the ways that Vars had betrayed the kingdom, from killing their father right up to drugging Lenore and locking her away. Lenore somehow managed to get angry about all the right things: about injustice in the kingdom, and poor people being hurt. There had been a brief period when Vars had managed that, but now... maybe his rising anger would be enough.

He took a step up onto the dais, and both Void and Verdant turned toward him, as if he were somehow interrupting. For a moment, he thought that he'd done the wrong thing by stepping forward like this. They stared at him, but then Void spoke, apparently certain now that he and Verdant had won their battle against the sorcerer. Vars could see why: Master Grey was down on one knee, obviously exhausted and in pain. The Hidden had struck every blow except the final one. Maybe they even wanted to put off that moment for their own ends.

"Is it done?" Void asked.

"Yes," Vars said, holding up the crown for him and Verdant to see. "It's done."

"Queen Lenore is dead?" Verdant asked.

Vars forced himself to nod. "She's dead."

The lie terrified him almost as much as the rest of it. He'd seen the powers of the Hidden, and if they could destroy Master Grey like this, there was no reason to think they couldn't reach into his mind in order to pick out truth from fiction.

Verdant moved closer to him, far too close for comfort, close enough that she could have touched him easily, yet she didn't. Her fingers were just above Vars's skin, and Vars suspected that one touch would be enough to send plants racing along his veins, bursting from him and killing him. She suspected something, she had to.

"How did you do it?" she whispered.

"I... knocked her out with the vial you gave me," Vars said. The words came out slower and more stumbling than he intended, sure that Verdant would see through him. "Then I... I cut her throat."

She was staring at him. She knew something was wrong, she had to.

"Oh, delicious," Verdant murmured. "A pity it couldn't last longer."

Vars almost sagged with relief as he realized then that she simply wanted to hear every detail of it, wanted to savor the violence of the

89

death. Void seemed to realize that too, because he snapped his fingers, taking Vars's attention from Verdant.

"Is that a sword made from star metal?" Void asked.

"It's the one the smith boy, Devin, made for my sister's wedding," Vars said. He took the opportunity to draw it, holding it up so that they could see it. It caught the light, shining blue-gray, runes standing out on its surface.

"A beautiful blade," Void said. "One worthy of slaying our foes. Go to the queen's sorcerer. Kill him."

"You want *me* to kill him?" Vars asked, swallowing. The moment was getting closer, little by little, and his fear was growing with that proximity. It felt like a huge wash of it inside him, caught behind a dam of his certainty, threatening to overflow at any moment and drown him.

"The symbolism is important," Void said. "The new king dismissing his sorcerer in a most... permanent way. He is weak, drained. End him, and we will crown you. Then, together, we will secure your kingdom against the threat it faces."

The dragons. The Hidden were offering to help against the dragons, and they probably had the power to do it. They were offering far more, too. Vars could be a king again, and could have the support of the most powerful mages in the kingdom. It was a combination that might make him powerful enough to rule everything. All he had to do was behead one old man he didn't even *like*.

Vars stepped off the dais, toward the spot where Master Grey still crouched on one knee, power spent. He stepped up next to the magus.

"All my life, I've been less," Vars said. "I've been the coward brother, the son no one wanted. I've been the one who had to take what he wanted, because no one would give it to me." He lifted the crown he'd taken from Lenore. It shone briefly in the light of the throne room. And he froze. He stood there, not able to do the next part, knowing what it would mean. He looked down at Master Grey, and found the old magus looking back up at him, understanding in his eyes.

"You can do this," Master Grey said. If it had just been those words, Vars might have stayed there still, but it wasn't. "We both can."

In that instant, Vars understood.

"I've been everything my siblings said I was," he said. "I don't want to be that man anymore."

It was time, and now that it came to it, Vars didn't feel frightened at all.

He threw the crown down at the feet of the Hidden, and it spun there like a top, or at least like a coin on a tabletop, slowly clattering toward a halt. The movement caught the eyes of the Hidden, and that was all Vars wanted from it. It gave him time to snatch up the vial that they'd given him and fling *that* at them, the way he'd flung the crown.

He watched the vial tumble perfectly across the space, seeming to hang there forever before it started to fall. It cracked into the stone of the dais and burst, the liquid within turning to gas on contact with the air. Vars saw the Hidden reel back from it, and knew that they must have breathed it in before they could stop themselves. For all their power, for all the twisted terror of the things they could do, there were still faces under those masks, and lungs to breathe in the vapor.

Even so, he couldn't leave this to chance. They weren't falling into unconsciousness the way Lenore had when he'd tried to get her to safety. Instead, they were merely moving with a sluggishness that made them seem as if they were mired in tar. Vars had seconds, at best, before they recovered.

He started to run for them.

Flowers and vines burst up around his feet, but the effects of the vapor had ruined Verdant's aim, so they grabbed a step behind his sprinting footfalls. This was where terror proved useful, driving Vars on with the kind of speed that knew that the real danger would come if he stopped. His feet ran over the wreckage of Master Grey's fallen stones, over the lip of the dais, bringing him into reach of the Hidden.

He'd never been the swordsman that Rodry had been, or had the subtle skill with weapons that Erin had. This didn't call for that, though; it just needed a sharp blade and a strong arm. Vars suspected that *this* blade was more than sharp enough for the job. Gripping the sword in two hands, he brought it up in two hands over his shoulder, then swung it round at Verdant's neck with all the force he could muster.

Time seemed to slow as Vars brought the blade around. The swing of it was perfect, a thing of deadly beauty that would connect with the Hidden's neck halfway and keep going. He could already feel the way he would turn the backswing into a thrust and drive it into Void's heart.

Then Void raised a hand and said a single word, laced with power.

"Fealty."

Vars's muscles locked in place so hard it was as if he had hit a wall. He froze in position, and the sheer impact of stopping like that *hurt*.

"A nice try," Void said, steadying himself against the throne. Vars struggled to move the sword he held, but couldn't. "If you hadn't sworn yourself to us, it might even have worked."

Vars fought against the control the Hidden had over him, flung himself against it with everything he had. Even as he did it, Void took the sword out of his hands as easily as he might have done with a child holding it, setting the blade down against the throne.

Verdant was already walking up in front of Vars, moving drunkenly with the effects of the vapor.

"You... you tried to *kill* me!" she said, and she made it sound like the worst betrayal there had ever been. "You promised to serve me, and you were going to kill me!"

She looked around to Void, and the leader of the Hidden gave the faintest of nods.

"We don't need him now," Void said.

Vars realized what they were going to do, but he couldn't have begun to run from it. This was one fate he had to face head on. Verdant reached out a hand, and vines, twigs, and thorns came together into a kind of spear made of natural things. She brought it back, and then thrust it forward with so much force that it punched Vars from his feet.

He flew back with the force of it, the spear going clean through him, and from the way his body screamed at him in agony, he knew it was a mortal blow. He tumbled back next to Master Grey, feeling his lifeblood pour from him.

It hurt. As Vars lay there, staring up at the ceiling, it felt as though living things were spreading from the impact point of the wound, spreading out, getting ready to kill him even if being stabbed didn't do it. He should have been terrified of that, of dying, of everything that came next. Instead, he found himself smiling.

Lenore was safe from them. He'd beaten them on *that* much, at least. He'd failed in so much else in his life, but in this, he'd won. He'd *won*.

CHAPTER EIGHTEEN

Master Grey watched Vars throw himself at the Hidden with all the fury that he might have expected from one of the young man's more warlike siblings. For a moment, he even knew hope as Vars made them reel back, and tried to strike at them with the star metal sword. There would have been a kind of neatness to it if Vars had been able to use that sword to end the threat, had stood up as the hero the kingdom needed in this moment.

Then the Hidden cut him down with the ease that came from twisted power. Void held him in place, while Verdant stabbed him with a weapon produced from her own vileness, flinging him back almost to where Grey was crouched. He looked up at Grey with something like an apology, but his failure to kill the Hidden didn't matter right then. He'd done the most important thing:

He'd bought Grey time.

Grey's lips moved in the words that would make for the last unbinding of his power. He felt himself grabbing for strands of it, pulling them in without even trying to balance them against the other forces of the world. It was like trying to hold on to the edge of a blade, but if Grey had one thing, it was willpower.

"It's time to end this," Void said, coming forward. Vars grabbed for his leg as he approached, trying to slow him, and Void simply stepped on his hand. Grey heard bone break. He didn't stop whispering the words of the unbinding. Every second Vars bought him was one second closer to being able to do this last thing.

Grey found himself thinking of all the other things he'd done in a long life devoted to magic and to the kingdom in equal parts. He'd done so much, and spent so much time and effort trying to protect the kingdom from the moment when the dragons would return to it. Now, though, he wasn't going to be there to see the ending to this.

Void and Verdant stood over Vars, looking down at him with obvious contempt. "It is a pity that our choice of king isn't going to work out, but that doesn't make a real difference. In the rubble of this kingdom, those with true power will always be able to find suitable puppets."

"I'll feed his body to the plants," Verdant said. "They'll grow the *prettiest* flowers with royal blood."

Grey drew in more power, and more beyond it, weaving it into rings around him, link after link put into place until he was sure that no one other than him could have held them all together. He wove that power into the middle of his being, linking it to everything he'd learned over the years, everything he'd bound in careful balance within him.

Void stood above him now. "I wonder what kind of fruit Verdant will grow in *your* corpse, magus."

"Fruit filled with power," Verdant said. "We will devour all you are, all you were, until there's nothing left."

"You think that you could hold all that is in me?" Grey said with a bitter laugh. "You think that you could survive one moment of it?"

He didn't rise from his crouched position. It hurt too much to do that.

"And yet you are the one on your knees," Void said. "So much time spent building up your precious balances, when all you had to do was take power from the right places."

"I have taken power from more places than you could imagine," Grey said. "I have held them down within myself. I have learned from the writings of the oldest sorcerers. I have learned skills you could not begin to fathom. I learned to see the world as it is, as it was, and as it might be. Here, let me show you."

He found himself thinking of all the lessons his teachers had taught him, all the ways they'd made him see the world to change it. He'd built layers of power into himself, bound them within, walled them behind careful boundaries.

He tore all those boundaries down now, ripping them apart with the power that he'd pulled in from around himself. Grey stood, blazing with power, screaming as the energy locked within him burned him from the inside. The power blazed from his eyes, from his hands, and he saw the Hidden reel back from it. The heat and the energy of it started to melt their precious masks from their faces, revealing features that seemed far too ordinary for beings of such horror. They stared at Grey in the realization of just how much power had been kept in check within him, looking at him with the fear that they so often inspired in other people. They turned as if they might run from it all, but there *was*

94

no running from this. The power blazed out and burned them, burned Vars, burned him, all at once.

Then the power within Grey exploded, and he knew no more.

*

The moment Lenore saw the power start to burst from Master Grey, she realized just how much danger she was in, standing in the great hall with the rest of them. She could feel the heat of it building, the energy of it blazing too bright to look at.

She looked around for a way out, but knew that there would be no way to get to the doors in time. If Master Grey was doing this, then he had to be sure that the Hidden in front of him weren't going to be able to escape. That meant that there was no time to waste; Lenore had to find a way to protect herself.

She grabbed for the tower shield that sat there above the niche, dragging it from its setting. She crouched behind the suit of armor that stood there, bringing the shield up in front of her for protection. Lenore was just in time, because she heard a blast ripple out, and a moment later she felt the impact of it against the shield, throwing her back into the niche.

The armor must have taken some of the blast, but it was also a weight that fell back on top of her, pinning her down as the power of the explosion Master Grey produced rippled out from him.

The roar of it was intense, the heat and the impact overwhelming. Lenore heard the rumble of stones falling, and again she could only hold the shield in place, feeling impact after impact striking it, battering at her. Lenore felt stones pour down on top of her, until the whole space around her was covered in them. Still, the shield held.

She hurt now from every small impact that had gotten past the shield, and there was a crushing weight pressing down on her as well. The space around her was dark, and Lenore almost panicked, assuming that she must be buried beneath the rubble of the hall. Had the whole castle fallen with the damage caused by Master Grey's explosion?

Lenore struggled against the weight atop her, pushing aside stones, and was both surprised and relieved to realize that at least some of the weight atop her was the suit of armor, which seemed to have fallen back off its stand on top of her. It was heavy, but that weight seemed to have helped it to protect Lenore from some of the other stones that had fallen in and around the niche she'd hidden in. Using the shield she held, she pushed aside the armor, wriggling out from underneath it and back into the light of the Great Hall.

The suit of armor had been partly melted by the explosion. There was rubble in the niche Lenore had sheltered in, while it filled large portions of the space within the Great Hall. There were large fallen stones there, and roofing beams, with parts of the ceiling now open holes that showed through to the floors of the castle above.

There was dust in the air, slowly settling, suggesting that perhaps Lenore hadn't been unconscious very long. Setting aside the tower shield, Lenore managed to pick her way out of the niche, into the broader space of the Great Hall. For a moment or two, it was impossible to make out the spot where Vars and the others had been standing, because it was obscured by rubble, the space around it blackened by the power of the blast, a beam fallen across it all.

Lenore made her way across to that rubble, as if somehow she might be able to help Master Grey or Vars there. She pulled aside stones, trying to find them, but the first bodies she found were not those of her brother or the royal sorcerer. The Hidden lay there, blasted and blackened, reduced to twisted things that barely seemed human anymore.

The melted remains of Void's mask lay a pace or two from his hand, still blank. His face had been damaged by the blast, but it looked more human, and more normal, than Lenore might have thought. Then, to her horror, she saw something else:

He was still moving.

Slowly, but surely, that twisted form was reaching out for his mask, as if it might help him. Maybe it might. Maybe there was power in it that Lenore didn't know about. She knew that she couldn't risk it.

She looked around until she found the sword that Devin had made for her and Vars had stolen. It lay fallen when one of the Hidden had killed him. Lenore took it up and stood over Void, staring down at him as he continued to reach for the mask.

"This is for my brother," she said, feeling anger lend her arm the strength it needed to drive the point of the blade down, through his skull. The leader of the Hidden cried out once, then went still. Lenore didn't know whether to feel satisfaction or relief at that.

Both of them were dead now, and they looked somehow smaller and weaker in death. When they'd been standing in front of Master

96

Grey, standing over him, they'd seemed so frightening and so powerful. Now, they just seemed ordinary. They didn't matter now. Lenore was more concerned about finding her brother.

There was no sign of Master Grey, but she found Vars beneath the rubble. She threw aside stones until she uncovered his body, still in death, damaged by the blast, and by the injuries the Hidden had inflicted on him.

The things he'd done made more sense to her now. He'd been trying to protect her when he'd shut her in the tower above. He'd taken her out of the way so that he could come back here, so that he could do... this.

Vars had sacrificed himself, and that seemed like the one thing Vars might never do. He'd gone up against the Hidden, and must have known the only way that act could end. He'd looked like a hero in that moment, and in spite of all the awful things he'd done in his life, Lenore found herself feeling grief for the loss of her brother. She cradled his body in her arms, feeling tears fall down onto his skin. She knew that Vars had killed their father, betrayed the kingdom, been responsible for so many other deaths, yet if he hadn't distracted the Hidden, would Master Grey have been able to finish that last, desperate spell?

Another impact reverberated around the Great Hall, and for a moment Lenore thought that maybe more fragments of it were going to fall as a consequence of Master Grey's spell. Then she realized that it must be the dragon attack, getting too close to the castle.

She laid her brother's still form back down on the floor of the Great Hall and forced herself to stand. Carefully, Lenore picked her way over to the throne. She picked up the crown first; it had a split in it now, but that didn't matter. She set it on her head, knowing that the people would need to see their queen. She sheathed the sword Devin had made at her side, too. It hadn't succeeded in killing the Hidden, but maybe it could do something against a dragon.

Something had to. Master Grey was dead, buried somewhere beneath the rubble, leaving no way to use magic against the attackers. Their preparations were insufficient, and now part of the castle had fallen to Master Grey's blast. Outside, the dragons were burning her city. Lenore sat on the throne, because it was hers, not theirs. She set the sheathed sword across her knees. If anyone, even dragons, wanted this throne, they would have to take it from her.

97

CHAPTER NINETEEN

Caught again. Erin worked at the bonds that held her as she walked, trying to find a way to loosen them, as they walked across the burning sand, but it turned out that Nicholas was good at tying people up. It was probably second nature for him, taking captives so that he could torture them horribly later. A man who wanted to be the next Ravin wouldn't do it out of anything as simple as mercy.

"There's no point trying to break free when you're surrounded by soldiers," Nicholas pointed out. He gestured to the dunes, too, as if to point out the futility of running off into a space with no water. For some reason only he knew, he was walking beside her now, like they were *friends* or something, rather than mortal enemies.

"You think I should wait until you've thrown me into the deepest dungeon you have in Sandport?" Erin shot back, but she gave up her attempt for now.

"What?" Nicholas asked. "You don't think that a monster like me is going to have you horribly executed the moment we arrive to make an example of you?"

"You're making fun of me?" Erin said. Bad enough that she'd fallen into the hands of her enemy, without him taunting her too. She tried to ignore him, but it was hard to do when she was stuck walking beside him all the way to Sandport, along a broken, stone-lined track. It didn't help that Nicholas was kind of hard to ignore in general; there was something about him that kept drawing her eye back to him, and not just to try to work out if there were any weak spots she could exploit to kill him. After a while, she couldn't keep herself from talking any longer.

"Why didn't you kill me?" Erin asked, as the path they were on started to climb up the space between two dunes.

"You'd rather I had?" Nicholas asked.

"I'm serious," Erin said. "Before, when I was trying to cut you down, you had me surrounded with archers. You could have had me killed, easily. Why not do it?"

"Maybe you're no use as a hostage if you're dead," Nicholas said. Somehow, though, Erin got the impression that wasn't the reason. There was more to it, and Nicholas... well, he wasn't anything like she'd expected. She'd expected someone more like Inedrin had been: brutish and cruel, callous even to the people who followed him. Instead, Nicholas seemed to inspire respect, even affection, in the people who served him.

"Not much further," Sarit, the desert warrior, said, approaching.

"Looking forward to getting the dust of the desert off you?" Nicholas asked him, and the other man laughed.

"As if the city has turned me as soft as you?"

To Erin's surprise, Nicholas laughed along with that. She suspected that Inedrin wouldn't have. She *knew* Ravin wouldn't. He would have killed the warrior, friend or not, for daring to suggest that he might have any hint of weakness.

"At least I'll be clean," Nicholas replied.

He confused Erin. So much of what she'd heard about him was about how he was trying to piece things back together, exactly the way a new Ravin might. About how he was ruthless with those who threatened his city. About how he was a strong leader, or a deadly warrior. The picture she'd had of him was of something very different from the man who was walking beside her now, who had let her escaping people go, and who had let her live even though he'd had every reason to kill her.

He didn't make sense to Erin, but apparently, she would have plenty of time to start to work him out in Sandport as his hostage, at least until she escaped. Maybe, when she did it, she'd find a way to bring him with her as *her* prisoner. Erin frowned at that thought, because she realized that she'd just envisioned not killing him, when that had been the whole point of heading so far south.

Erin was still thinking about that when they finished climbing a dune and Sandport came into view below.

It was a strange place by every standard Erin knew. She was used to the rivers of Royalsport, yet here, there wasn't the water for it. Instead, sand blew through the streets, piled here and there against the sides of buildings, but mostly swept away from them in what must have taken a constant effort.

Its focal point seemed to be a central market so full of stalls that it was almost like a city within the city, so many traders there that Erin couldn't even begin to imagine the places they all must have come from. Caravans looked as though they were set to leave the city, although none were at the moment. There were other squares too, set around the city, and it took Erin a moment to work out that each was set around a central well, water apparently precious in a place with so little of it.

There were square-sided barracks there within the city, and drill squares beyond it for the soldiers of the city to train in. Most of the other buildings were more elegant, even the poorest of them having a simple beauty to their white walls and flat roofs. More expensive buildings rose above them, some with spires, others domes, most gilded or painted to show off the wealth of those within. Erin could pick out the palace there, which was more like a broad central tower, rising to a pinnacle high above the city. There seemed to be no plan to the layout, streets apparently formed wherever people had felt like building their homes.

All of it was enough to catch Erin's eye, but not to hold it, because there was something far more immediate to do that: a battle was raging in front of the walls of the city. Hundreds of men on both sides clashed out on the sands, hacking at one another with swords while arrows filled the air above. Even from here Erin could hear the screams and the clash of blades. She could also make out the large, familiar form toward the rear of the battle, directing one force from a platform that looked something like a mobile castle, defended on every side by his men.

"Inedrin," Nicholas said, and there was real hatred in his voice.

"He must have heard that you were out of your city," Erin said. "That ambush back there was designed to slow you down."

"So that I would come back to find my city already fallen," Nicholas agreed. "He wouldn't even have to kill me, just block my return and let the heat of the sands do the rest. Sarit, Ankari, to me!"

His friends ran over, and it seemed that any lightheartedness that had been there before was gone now.

"It looks like Ferrent is holding things," Ankari said.

"For now," Sarit replied. "Look at the way his lines are getting overstretched. Why has he decided to fight outside the city walls, rather than setting up for a siege?"

100

Erin could guess at the reason for that. "Inedrin will have lured him out," she said. "He'll have made it look like he was weak, and your friend could destroy him easily."

Sarit gave her a hard look, and then turned to Nicholas. "We're including prisoners in the planning now?"

"When the prisoner is the one who killed Ravin, yes," Nicholas said. "And I agree with her. Ferrent is straightforward. He would have seen Inedrin out on the ground before the city and seen a chance to end this without any of us being in danger, and without threatening the city. You know he's like a mother hen."

"Fat hen," Sarit said. "Hen that's about to get its neck wrung."

Down below, Erin could see the truth of that. The forces of the city had come out too far from the walls. Inedrin's forces were starting to encircle them. If they managed it completely, they could stop the forces of the city from being able to retreat and kill every one of them.

"We need to help them," Ankari said.

Erin looked around the small force there. It had been more than enough to ambush her crew, but compared to the full might of Inedrin's army, it was like a drop in the ocean.

"If you run down there without a plan, the battle will swallow you up without even chewing," Erin said. She didn't know why she was helping them like this, except that if it came to a choice between Nicholas and Inedrin, she knew which was the worse option.

"So what do you suggest, invader?" Sarit asked.

Nicholas was looking at her. "Yes, Erin, what *do* you suggest to save my people?"

Erin was a little caught off guard by that. She hadn't expected that they would actually listen to her in a moment like this. If she'd been in their position, she would have assumed that she was trying to find a way to get them all to kill one another. Maybe that was even a good idea. If she could give them a plan that would kill both Nicholas and Inedrin, the world might be a safer place for it.

If Nicholas had just asked for a way to kill his enemies, she might even have been able to do that. As it was, though, he'd asked for a way to help the people of his city. He really did want to protect them above all else. So Erin told the truth.

"See the way Inedrin has positioned himself at the back of his army?" she said. "It means the force from the city can't get to him, but you could. If this is really about who gets to rule, then if you kill him, his forces have no reason to keep fighting."

"That is exactly what I was thinking," Nicholas said, and Erin realized that this had been some kind of test. He knew exactly as well as her what was required. Erin saw him lean close to Ankari and whisper something.

"You're sure?" the woman asked.

He nodded, and she headed off in the direction of one of the horses.

"Sarit," Nicholas said. "Have the men form up. We are going to be an arrowhead fired at Inedrin's heart."

"Yes, my lord," Sarit said. He turned and went to the men, calling out orders over the sounds of the battle below.

"The question is what we do with you," Nicholas said to Erin. "I suppose I *could* leave you here with Ankari to watch you."

"You think your wise woman can keep me from running off?" Erin asked. To her surprise, Nicholas gestured to the sands around them. "If you want to run, run. Better you do it now than you hurt one of my people along the way."

Erin thought about it, she really did, but she could see in Nicholas's eyes that he was hoping she would do something else.

"What's the alternative?" Erin asked.

Nicholas reached close to her, and now there was a knife in his hand. He slashed the ropes that held Erin, leaving her to grit her teeth as blood flowed back into her hands.

"You help us," Nicholas said. Ankari was back beside them then, and to Erin's surprise, she had Erin's short, long-bladed spear. The woman passed it to her, and Erin snatched it from her hands, grateful for the weight of it once again.

"You realize that I could just stab you with this?" Erin said to Nicholas.

"You could try," Nicholas agreed. He jerked his head in the direction of Inedrin. "Or you could use it on someone who deserves it far more. I'm told you have a knack for killing tyrants."

Erin gripped the spear tightly, trying to think. Not that there was much to think *about*. There was a battle in front of her, and if her side didn't win, she would be as much at Inedrin's mercy as anyone else. She guessed that she could always stab Nicholas after.

"All right," she said. "I'll help."

102

"Good," Nicholas said. He led her to the spot where his men were forming a wedge of soldiers. "Are you ready?"

Erin nodded. "I'm ready."

"Good." Nicholas drew his sword. "Then let's do this. Charge!"

CHAPTER TWENTY

Nicholas led the charge down toward the rear of Inedrin's forces, sword held high, feet pounding on the hard-packed sand of the desert floor. For the first few paces, fear rose within him that Erin might strike him down even then, but for now at least, it seemed that she was content to charge beside him.

The excitement and fear that came with battle rose within him, and Nicholas fought it down. He had to think clearly, had to focus.

The battle raged below, and Nicholas could make out Ferrent now, at the heart of the city's forces, cutting this way and that with a two-handed sword while around him enemies swarmed like ants. He had a spear sticking from his side, but it didn't seem to be stopping him. The cacophony of the battle grew as they got closer, until everything else seemed drowned out by the ring of steel and the cries of pain.

At first the chaos below was so great that it seemed Inedrin's men didn't even notice the small force charging at them from behind. That was good; every step they could close without being spotted was another moment in which their enemy couldn't mount a defense against their assault. The less time they had, the less chance there was of them being able to hurt Nicholas's people.

They made it about halfway there before some of Inedrin's people started to turn and point at them. They started to form up, moving to block the way between Nicholas and Inedrin's battle tower. Nicholas's heart clenched at that sight, because this was the crucial moment.

"Don't stop!" Nicholas called out. He didn't know if his voice managed to carry over the noise of the battle or not, but he had to try. "Getting to Inedrin is *everything*."

The others roared out something that might have been agreement, but might have just been a battle cry, and then they were slamming into the enemy, cutting their way through.

Nicholas hit that first wall of defenders, kicking one man aside and cutting down a second with his curved blade. He took the impact of a sword on his long knife, and then he was past, the enemy formation falling apart as everything turned to the unpredictable violence of individual battles. Beside him, he saw Erin plunge her spear into a man's throat, leap over the swipe of a sword, and keep running forward.

"Keep going!" Nicholas called out. It was impossible not to give in to the adrenaline rush of the battle now. He hacked a web of sword strokes in front of himself that forced men back from him, and it didn't matter if those blows connected or not; all that mattered was creating enough space to get through.

Around him, his people plunged into the battle, the weight of their wedge punching a hole in the enemy's lines. Nicholas saw Sarit hacking at foes with short axes, while even Ankari seemed to have joined the fight, striking out with daggers and then darting away before anyone could catch her.

Erin was like the onslaught of a storm. She seemed to bounce from enemy to enemy, and everywhere her spear touched, men died. There was a wild abandon to her attacks that Nicholas could have stood and watched forever, except that he had his own fighting to do, as he was reminded sharply when an axe came at his head. Nicholas blocked it with both sword and dagger, kicked the wielder hard enough to double him over, and cut his head from his shoulders.

He kept going, and the deeper they got into the battle, the fewer of his people Nicholas had beside him, caught up in their own desperate fights, slowed by the simple friction of the battlefield. Nicholas couldn't watch for them, though, couldn't let his fears for them distract him; the tower from which Inedrin was giving commands was getting closer with every heartbeat, and Nicholas knew that he couldn't stop to wait for the others. If he stopped, he would be stuck there, and eventually, the weight of numbers would overwhelm him. He kept pushing forward with Erin and just a few of his guards for protection.

Somewhere across from them, he could see the fight for the city continuing. Ferrent was no longer visible in it all, but he could make out Sarit cutting down a pair of men, and saw Ankari with a bow she had obviously stolen from one of the fallen, sending arrow after arrow into their foes. In spite of their efforts, the enemy forces seemed to be getting perilously close to completing their encircling of Nicholas's troops. He kept moving.

Close to it, Nicholas could see that the war tower was little more than a quartet of carts with an improvised structure built above it. Like Inedrin himself, it seemed more impressive than it was. Nicholas slammed into the men guarding it, cutting one down with a backhand sweep of his sword, parrying a blow on the follow-through, and stabbing a man with the dagger he held. Beside him, Erin stabbed a man who got too close to her, and then leapt at the tower as if she might climb it like a cat. To Nicholas's astonishment, she actually found purchase on the improvised structure, starting to haul herself up hand over hand.

Cursing to himself, Nicholas followed, trying to keep up. He wasn't anywhere near as light as Erin, but he managed to find a grip on the tower nevertheless, pulling himself up hand over hand. He could feel the structure of the thing shaking as he rose, obviously not designed for more than one occupant at the top. Still, he kept climbing.

The tower was shuddering alarmingly now as Nicholas and Erin climbed it. Inedrin's people had done their best, but they'd clearly only been able to create so much given the materials available. It meant that Inedrin could loom over his forces, and seem like a leader without ever coming close to the front, but it was anything but stable. Nicholas had to jam his knife in between two slats of wood just to keep his grip on the thing, rising ever higher.

He could see Inedrin peering over the edge now, a huge man with an even larger axe in his hands, a crown on his head as if he already ruled the whole of the Southern Kingdom. He glared down at Nicholas and seemed to recognize him even as he hung there, trying to keep his grip.

"Die, pretender!" Inedrin bellowed, and swung down at Nicholas, so that Nicolas had to swing out from the tower to avoid it, keeping his grip with just one hand. He heard the splintering impact of the great axe against the wooden structure, and maybe it was that, or maybe it was just how much weight was all leaning in one direction, but the war tower started to topple.

Nicholas saw Erin leap clear, and a second later he followed her example, pushing himself free from the falling structure and tumbling in a roll as he hit the ground to absorb some of the impact. Even so, the jolt of it was enough to knock the air from his lungs. He struggled to rise and draw his blade to get back into the fight, seeing Inedrin staggering from the wreckage of his tower.

One of his men was standing over Nicholas then, a blade already raised to slash down at him. As stunned as he was, Nicholas knew he wouldn't be able to move aside from the blow in time. He could already see the sword starting its descent, and when the blow was finished, he had no doubt that he would be dead.

The tip of a spear appeared through the soldier's throat as Erin stabbed him from behind, red with his blood. The soldier gave a gasp, and the sword he held fell from his fingers as Erin tossed him aside. She stood over Nicholas then, and it occurred to him that it would be easy for her to stab down now and finish this. No one would be any the wiser. They would all think that one of Inedrin's men had done it.

Instead, she reached down a hand and helped him to his feet.

"Come on," she said, using her spear to point in the direction Inedrin had staggered. "We aren't done yet."

They started after him, but already, Inedrin's men were starting to regroup after the impact of the tower, forming a wall of flesh between Nicholas, Erin, and their leader. There had to be at least a dozen men there in the way; too many for the two of them to hope to fight at once.

Arrows sang out, thudding into the men there. Nicholas saw people charge forward, and it took him a second to recognize the ones who had been his prisoners alongside Erin. The five of them rushed Inedrin's men, striking out with a variety of scavenged weapons, and it took Nicholas a moment to realize that he should be helping. He charged into the fray, cutting down one of Inedrin's troops, then another, while Erin plunged her spear into a man's chest, then kicked him free.

In seconds, the wall of troops in their way was no more. The only problem was that Nicholas found himself surrounded by his former captives. A young man with a slender blade leveled it at his heart, while a woman kept an arrow trained on him.

"Say the word, Erin, and we'll finish this."

Nicholas could only stand there, looking over at Erin.

"No," she said, after what seemed like a heart-stopping couple o seconds. "He isn't the threat here. Inedrin is."

Her people lowered their weapons. Even if they didn't look happy about it, they followed her orders.

"What are you doing here?" Erin asked them.

"You didn't think we would just leave you, did you?" the tribesman with them asked.

"We followed you, looking for a way to break you free," th woman said. "We... damn it. More of them!"

There were indeed more of Inedrin's troops coming up behind them. Nicholas could see Erin getting ready to fight them, but he put a hand on her arm.

"The way to Inedrin is clear," he said. "The way to finish this is to kill him."

"Do it," the woman with the bow said. "We'll hold them here."

Nicholas grabbed Erin's arm and pulled her in the direction Inedrin had gone, and soon they were running, chasing the big man as he limped to safety, dragging his axe behind him.

He turned as they approached, giving a roar like a wounded bear.

"Time to die," he snarled, and swung his axe around with more speed than its weight suggested was possible. Nicholas barely danced back from it in time.

Inedrin went to follow up, but Erin's spear was there, threatening to skewer him if he did. He turned his attention to her, and Nicholas swung a sword blow at his head that the big man barely parried.

He was quick for a large man, and clearly knew how to use the axe he carried. Nicholas wasn't sure that he would have been able to beat this man in single combat, because every blow he swung felt like a hammer ringing against his blade, and every counter Nicholas tried found itself parried.

He wasn't alone, though; Erin was there, and that changed *everything*. Nicholas found himself moving in concert with her, spreading out so that Inedrin couldn't attack one of them without exposing himself to the other. It felt natural to fall into the rhythm of her steps, fighting in the spaces she left, in a dance as intricate as any courtly one. Nicholas struck low and she struck high without being told. He feinted left, and she struck into the opening as Inedrin went with it. The big man accumulated small wounds on his arms and legs one after another.

He got his retaliation for those wounds, though. Nicholas saw the butt of Inedrin's axe strike Erin's stomach, and he barely distracted him with a stroke of the sword in time. Another blow came at his chest so fast and hard that Nicholas could barely strike it flat with his sword, the weighted head of the axe still hitting him like a hammer. He and Erin circled warily.

Inedrin charged at Erin then, obviously hoping to take her out of the fight and turn back to Nicholas. He aimed a sweeping blow at her that Nicholas knew would cut through her spear like kindling. It shouldn't have made a difference, but he knew he couldn't let that happen. Cursing, he did the only thing he could think of: he threw himself forward, crossing his knife and sword between him and Inedrin to take the blow.

The steel of his weapons absorbed some of it, and his armor took more, so he wasn't cut in half. Even so, Nicholas felt the head of the axe bite into his side, sharp and agonizing. He clamped down on that head, stopping Inedrin from pulling it clear.

Erin struck the leader of his enemies through the chest with her spear, driving him down to one knee. As he lost his grip on his axe, Nicholas was able to pull back from it, lift his sword, and bring it round in a sweep that met Inedrin's neck halfway. His head bounced from his shoulders, his body collapsing onto the sand.

Nicholas felt like doing the same, but Erin was there, holding him up, his arm around her shoulders. She didn't seem to understand when Nicholas started for the head, but when he grabbed it and lifted it, she seemed to get what he was doing.

"Inedrin is dead!" Nicholas bellowed, loud enough that it carried even over the noise of the closest fights. Those slowed, and stopped, men looking to the head he held, then repeating his message in a ripple across the battlefield. "Your leader has fallen! You could keep fighting, but why? The man who would rule you is gone, and I have no quarrel with you. Join me, and you will have a place in my kingdom. Fight against me, and I will cut you down as I did your lord!"

For a moment, he thought they might not do it. It would only take one of them to rise and proclaim himself Inedrin's successor, and the battle would start again. The terror of that rose in Nicholas, and he had to fight to keep any sign of it off his face.

If this were another kind of conflict, it would never have worked. Yet it was what it was: a clash between two men who wanted the crown. Now that one lay dead, the reason for it was gone. Slowly, one by one, weapons tumbled to the ground, and the fear Nicholas had felt before turned to triumph.

"You did it," Erin whispered to him.

"*We* did it," Nicholas corrected her.

CHAPTER TWENTY ONE

Anders hadn't felt power like this before. All his life, he'd known that he was powerful, that he was special. He'd known that he had the talent for using magic. He'd known that he was from a good family, that he would have every advantage in life. He'd even known that he had a destiny, one that made him simply more special than anyone else in the world.

All of that paled into insignificance compared to the power that came from riding atop Shadr, commanding a force of dragons and their creatures. From here, Anders had the power to grant life or death. He could control the world, or order it burned. Every wingbeat was filled with the power that Shadr held, and because Anders controlled her, *he* was the one who commanded that power.

"I could order you to do anything," Anders whispered, and the dragon's voice susurrated back in his mind.

If you weaken, I will kill you.

Anders knew he wouldn't weaken. He was chosen for this. Even so, he kept tight control over Shadr, not trying to extend it directly over the dragons who followed her. With her under his command, he didn't need to.

He could feel the dragon's anger and hatred toward the world. That was fine, because it matched all the feelings of betrayal that had run inside Anders ever since he'd learned that Master Grey had chosen another to be the one to fulfill his destiny. The anger he felt at losing so many friends for this came out then, Shadr roaring in response to it, blasting out flames into the air in front of them.

Your anger almost matches me, Shadr whispered in his mind.

They ate away the landscape beneath them. The creatures swarming beneath couldn't keep up, but that didn't matter. The dragons around Anders were more than enough to do what he wanted.

What he wanted seemed uncertain, possibilities swirling around his head until he couldn't pick them apart. He wanted to rule the kingdom and to destroy it, to make people bow down to him and to watch them burn, to take his rightful place as king of all of it and to burn it all to ashes so that he could start again.

"I'm not a fool," Anders said. "I can feel you trying to influence me."

Then break the connection between us.

Anders shook his head. "The amulet gives me the power. I'm the one in control here."

To prove it, he pointed at a patch of ground where buildings rose up in a hamlet. A pair of dragons swooped down at Shadr's command, wings tucked so that they plummeted toward their target. They opened them again as they got lower, moving into a glide, and their mouths opened wide, flames pouring forth in a torrent.

Anders watched the houses go up like torches, black smoke pouring from them as the flames consumed everything within them. *This* was real power, and soon, he would show Royalsport that power in earnest.

*

Royalsport came into view, and the first thing Nerra saw was the flames. They raged around the outer city, smoke rising up above it. Nerra could make out the swarming ranks of the Lesser there below, forming a ring around the city, while above... above, the dragons flew.

We can stop this, Alith promised her.

Still, it was impossible for Nerra to ignore her fear as she watched the ones Shadr had sent. They swooped back and forth, breathing lines of fire that struck at people and buildings below. The slums of the outer city were ablaze, people out in the streets, trying to fight the flames with bucket chains and weary effort. They scattered each time one of the dragons dove at them, only to come back each time to try to defend their homes from the flames. Nerra saw people fighting the Lesser in the streets, while siege weapons on the walls fired at the dragons who got too close.

Even so, there was damage to the main city. Nerra saw flames pour down across one of the rivers there, filling the air above with steam. One of the towers of the House of Scholars had collapsed under impact from a dragon, while the House of Merchants seemed to be ablaze. It was strange, seeing the city she had called home so nearly destroyed, both a moment for grief and one for determination. Nerra couldn't let this keep going.

The dragons banked this way and that, each of them working to cause maximum terror, but Nerra could see a chance in that.

"They're just working alone without Shadr to command them," she said. "If we strike at them in formation, we can pick them off."

We will strike as one, Alith agreed.

Their flight of dragons divided up into trios, each one flying at one of the dragons terrorizing the city. Nerra pointed Alith at one of them, a large green dragon, and Alith climbed, getting above it.

We will pin them between us and the ground, Alith sent, as they climbed higher. *Wait... wait... now!*

She and the two dragons flanking her dove at the green dragon, which was too busy trying to burn buildings below to spot them at first. When it did look up, it shrieked and tried to bank away, but the two that were diving with them broke to either side, hemming it in. That left Alith, diving straight at her foe.

The green dragon breathed poison up at them, but Alith rolled in midair, avoiding the cloud of it. Her own mouth opened wide, and lightning crackled from it, striking their foe on the flank. It roared in pain as the energy crackled across it, and that moment of pause let Alith slam into it, claws and teeth extended. For a moment, they snapped and snarled at one another, and it was all Nerra could do to cling to her back. She found her claws having to dig into Alith's scales as she found herself upside down, hanging above the world below.

Then Alith's claws tore into the wings of her foe, taking away the one thing that held it aloft, sending it plummeting down to slam into the buildings of the city. It started to crawl away, but then there were human guards there, hacking at it with axes and swords.

Nerra shouted in elation at that brief moment of victory, but Alith was already regrouping with the others she flew with, turning toward another of the dragons there. They flew for it, and in that moment, Nerra saw one of the siege weapons swing her way.

"Alith, *turn!*"

The dragon did it almost as fast as Nerra could say it, turning away as a long spear from one of the ballistae flew past them. Of course the people below had no way of knowing which dragons were which. They could only see great, ferocious beasts locked in a battle for the sky.

We should stay clear of them. Their stinging weapons will harm us.

"If the other side fly too close, we'll have to go close too," Nerra insisted. "We just have to hope that they realize we're trying to help."

They went for another dragon, three of them descending on it all at once. That dragon wheeled away before they could get to it, but even so, that meant it was moving away from the city, so that it couldn't do more harm until it came around again.

"It's working!" Nerra called to Alith.

Working together, we can defeat them.

Around them, fights were continuing between her dragons and the ones Shadr had sent, the sky alive with flames and lightning, frost and the flash of claws. Nerra heard the roars of dragons striking out in anger and reeling back in pain. Alith herself dove, sweeping down low over the lesser, letting loose another blast of lightning that swept them from her path. Powerful wingbeats took her skyward again, up among those who fought with her.

The ones who followed Alith had the upper hand now. They'd struck while the others were still focusing on attacking the city, and they were working together where the other dragons had split apart to cause maximum terror. It meant that several dragons were already tumbling from the sky, falling down onto the city, some dead, some wounded enough that the humans below could strike at them with the weapons they held.

Nerra didn't know what to feel as she saw that. A part of her was elated that they were winning, that they were able to save the people below from the threat that they faced. Another part of her had seen how intelligent and how powerful these creatures were, and she felt sorrow when they fell like sparrows from the sky, the ground shaking every time one of them impacted on the ground below. This had to happen, though. They had to win this, before…

Nerra felt the pressure on the edge of her mind, in a familiar presence that made her look around. Even though the shapes on the horizon were far from them all, Nerra could make out the dark shape at the front all too easily. Shadr was coming, and she was getting closer.

A second force of dragons came with her, powering forward on wide wings. As Nerra saw them coming, several of her dragons turned to face them, their best hope to slow them long enough to defeat the first force before they turned to face the second.

There was no time for that, though. This new flight of dragons came on with thunderous intensity, flame searing the ground before them, roaring voices striking terror. They came forward, slamming into the dragons who moved to intercept them with utter ferocity. Nerra saw

113

Shadr slam into one, tearing and rending with knife like teeth until it fell limp from the sky. More dragons poured in, and Nerra knew that there was no way they could just charge into this new mass.

"We need a new plan," she said.

What plan can there be? Alith asked.

Nerra looked at the city, at the height of its buildings, and at the siege weapons that were still sending bolts and stones up into the sky.

"We have to take them somewhere it's dangerous to follow," she said. "Call the others back. We need to fight them close to the city."

Alith must have sent the signal, because those facing Shadr and her dragons pulled back. Not all of them made it. Nerra saw one caught by a blast of shadow as it turned, another dragged down by a copper-scaled beast that clung to its prey as it fell.

As Shadr got closer, Nerra's eyes widened as she saw a figure there upon her back. The great black dragon wheeled, giving Nerra a better view of the creature that sat there, clinging to Shadr's scales. She had expected it to be another of the Perfected, but there was no shine of scales on this one, no lizard-like form atop Shadr's back. Instead, the figure looked human, and that could only mean one thing:

The amulet bearer, the one they'd tried to kill, was there with Shadr.

CHAPTER TWENTY TWO

Devin could see that battle now, like a storm filling the sky over Royalsport. The breaths of more dragons than Devin could count flashed out, lighting up the sky with flame and lightning, frost and acid in searing bursts. Their roars sounded like thunder, the noise only growing as they got closer.

We are close, Memnir assured him. *I can feel them, and their so-called queen. I will tear them from the sky. I will put a stop to this... foolishness.*

Devin could only hope that was true. But then, why would Master Grey have sent him to find the old dragon if there wasn't some way for that to change the course of things? Devin had to believe that there was a reason he and Renard were riding the most ancient dragon alive into the midst of battle.

He urged Memnir to greater speed with every wingbeat, trying to catch up with the dragons they were following, but the truth was that there was only so much speed that the ancient dragon had to give. Each wingbeat seemed to take an eternity, even if the power of the creature left Devin and Renard clinging to Memnir's back for dear life.

Devin had been in plenty of fights by now, had even seen the last dragon attack on Royalsport, but none of it was even close to this. It wasn't just the scale of it, the sky full of such a mass of fighting, writhing dragons that there seemed almost no room for the light beyond. It was that it was a very different way of fighting too. Where armies of men might slam into one another in a vicious, pushing press, this battle was a thing of chases and sudden dives, striking and wheeling away, with brief close bursts of violence as dragons bit and clawed at one another like tangling eels.

"What's the plan?" Renard called from behind Devin. "Please tell me that there's actually a plan."

We find the queen, we strike her down, and we command the others to cease, Memnir whispered in Devin's mind. He didn't bother relaying that to Renard, though, because he doubted that it would reassure the thief.

115

"Just hold on," Devin said instead.

Memnir's slow, languorous flight propelled them forward into the battle. Flames burst around them, the air crackling with the heat as dragons breathed death at their enemies. Bolts and stones came up from ground level too, fired by the defenders seemingly at random, since there were no uniforms up here, and there was no way to tell the warring sides apart.

A dragon came at them, and to Devin's surprise, Memnir craned his great neck around, blasting the oncoming foe with a burst of frost that made it shriek and wheel away. Memnir banked then, with slow and stately grace, going down low over the city, and Devin could feel him hunting steadily for his foe while smaller dragons flitted around the tallest buildings.

I was fighting when these younglings were still in their eggs, the dragon rumbled.

One foe came at them, streaking forward with all the speed and strength of youth. Devin could feel the difference as Memnir turned, far too slowly. The younger dragon slammed into his side, and Devin felt the pain as much as heard the dragon's roar of agony. The two dragons plunged down toward the ground, the smaller one pulling away, and Memnir spread his vast wings wide, trying to slow their descent. The dragon still tumbled clumsily through the air, now so close to the rooftops below that Devin had to cling tightly to the dragon to avoid being struck by one of the chimney stacks.

A cry came from behind him, and Devin looked back to see Renard tumbling off along the top of one of the roofs. Apparently, he hadn't been as good at dodging chimney stacks as Devin. He saw Renard tumble over and over toward the edge of the roof, his hand barely clamping onto the guttering in time. Devin saw him hanging there, swinging his legs to try to get back onto the tiles.

"Renard has fallen off!" Devin called out to Memnir. "We need to go back for him!"

Why would we want the extra weight? the dragon grumbled. *He will be safer on the ground.*

That was probably true, given the bloody chaos above. Devin saw dragons tearing at one another with reddened claws and dagger-like teeth, rending one another's flesh and sending each other tumbling from the sky. Those who fell on the open ground beyond the city plowed great furrows in it as they fell, while those slain over the city

116

crushed its buildings, sending up showers of stone and wood as they impacted upon it. People ran screaming in every direction, or tried to finish off those dragons that were merely wounded, not dead.

"Memnir, above you!" Devin called, as he saw the dragon that had struck them before wheeling around for another pass.

The ancient dragon turned, and this time he was able to wheel to face his foe. Memnir breathed out magic, and Devin could feel the power of it as the dragon shaped it. He could feel the skill behind it, and he lent his own strength to Memnir's efforts. Shards of ice shot from the dragon's mouth, and it was like a hundred spears of it shot out to strike the dragon that had come for them. Some of those shards shattered on the dragon's scales, but many more did not, piercing the onrushing creature and sending it crashing down toward the ground.

Devin felt a brief moment of elation, but he could feel how much effort it had taken for the dragon to do that much damage. With the wound on his side, Memnir seemed to be flying slower now, unable to climb high again, proceeding over the city at an almost sedate pace. Even so, Memnir seemed determined to throw himself back into the fight.

Fires raged over the city, and Devin directed the great dragon's attention to them for a moment. Memnir breathed out frost in the direction of the nearest one, so that the cold and the water of it damped down the flames and turned them just to steam. With the fires reduced like that, the people of the city were able to run out and finish the job using buckets and water taken from the rivers of the city, which seemed to be running high now, rushing through Royalsport in a way that would have kept out another kind of army.

Instead, the dragons kept flying over it all, setting light to more of it even as Memnir put out some of the largest fires with his breath.

Waiting will not gather my strength, the dragon informed him. *Time has been too cruel to me. I wane as my age returns to me.*

Devin had known that the dragon was old, but he'd assumed that the weakness he'd been able to feel in Memnir had been something that would pass. Instead, if he concentrated now, he could feel the steady dripping away of power from the creature, and if what Memnir told him was true, it meant that they only had a short time to do everything they needed to here.

Devin looked around until he spotted the target they sought, picking out Anders's form atop a huge dragon with scales of the deepest black.

117

That is Shadr, Memnir explained. *I can feel her thoughts, her commands. I can feel the magic of the amulet there, as well.*

"We need to stop them," Devin said. He saw the black dragon circle wide of the city, throwing out what looked like deepest shadow at one of the dragons engaged in the fight there. The dragon that the shadows struck shrieked in apparent pain and fell back, wheeling off with one wing injured.

We do, Memnir agreed. *As long as Shadr flies, her forces will not stop attacking. She must die, and the amulet must be taken.*

He banked slowly around to line up with their target, and now the huge span of his wings started to beat in earnest. Memnir drove forward with Devin upon his back, and now, it seemed that the ancient dragon was moving with greater speed, ready to throw everything he had into one last, great, titanic battle.

He was still powering forward when a bolt from a ballista tore through the membrane of one of his wings. Devin cursed as the dragon lurched to the side, seeming to right himself with an effort. Memnir clung to the sky with an effort, but weakened as he was by the impact of the bolt, he had no way to avoid the rushing onslaught of another of Shadr's dragons.

This one was a shining, burnished silver, and struck at Memnir from above, so that if the ancient dragon had stayed level, Devin would have been directly in the line of their attacker's extended claws. As it was, though, Memnir turned in midair, rolling belly up so that he could strike with all four claws at once.

Devin felt the impact of the silver dragon slamming into Memnir, and he was barely able to cling onto the ancient dragon's scales, hanging there the way he might have done from an overhanging rock. Only *this* handhold bucked and shifted in the midst of aerial combat, wings flexing, claws lashing out. Memnir rolled up above his foe, and Devin saw its maw bloodied with Memnir's flesh. Then Memnir opened his mouth and blasted the other dragon full in the face with all the force of his icy breath. The other dragon shrieked and tumbled down, already dead before it hit the ground.

Memnir was losing height too, though. Whatever wounds he'd sustained, Devin could feel the dragon's lifeblood leaching out of him, could feel his pain through the link between them.

I fear that they have killed me, Memnir whispered in Devin's mind.

"No," Devin said. "You can't. We have a destiny to finish."

118

Destinies can be… complicated things, the dragon replied, and started to plummet. He was facing the city, and started to fall into it. His wings were spread wide, but one had been made ragged by the impact of the ballista bolt, and it meant that there was no way for Memnir to arrest their rapid descent.

They were at the level of the highest rooftops now, and Devin felt the impact of a tower against one of Memnir's flanks, stone giving way even as it bounced the dragon away, his tumble continuing. Devin found himself pressed flat against Memnir as he fell, trying to keep his grip, while he looked for any way to help with this.

They scraped along a rooftop, ripping slates and timbers from it. Memnir kept going down an alley, flanks scraping along the buildings on either side. The dragon shrieked in a last, dying call that almost deafened Devin. Then they hit the ground, scraping along it, plowing a furrow through the cobblestones that sent them flying up around Devin's face.

Devin found himself thrown clear of the dragon, slamming against a wall and then falling down along it. He hit cobbles and rolled, but that didn't take enough of the impact out of it. Devin felt something break in his side as he skidded along the cobbles, then bounced from them, one after another, every part of his body bruising. Something clipped his head, and Devin's vision swam.

He saw Memnir scrape to a halt, body twisted by the impacts with the cobbles. The dragon lay there, far too still, and already, people were pouring out of the buildings around Devin, rushing at Memnir with every weapon they could find.

"No!" Devin yelled. "He's… he's on our side!"

It was too late, though; Memnir was dead even without the efforts of the people of the city. Devin could feel the moment when the connection between them broke, like an empty room somewhere inside of him that had briefly been full of life. The pain of the dragon's loss was sudden, and tinged with guilt. After all, Devin had been the one to draw him into this.

Devin had more physical pains, too. He hurt in ways worse than he could ever remember hurting, and could barely manage to stand. Yet he had to. Above him, the battle still raged.

Determined to help, Devin limped on into the city.

CHAPTER TWENTY THREE

Nerra and Alith surged through the sky, plunging toward Shadr and her human rider. The great black dragon twisted away from the flash of their lightning, fired back shadows, and now it was Alith who had to barrel roll away from the attack, the cold of Shadr's breath palpable on Nerra's skin as the shadows got too close.

They swept past one another, turned like two knights jousting in the lists, and came back at one another again. Lightning met shadow in another burst of breath, and they followed it with flames as they passed one another, each trying to catch their foe unaware. Nerra clung to Alith's back as she rolled away from that second blast, the sky spinning around her so that for a moment, Nerra didn't know which way was up.

You are worthless, you are weak.

The words sounded inside Nerra's skull, and she couldn't shut them out. Shadr was close enough now that Nerra could feel the dragon's presence inside her mind no matter how much she tried to block it. Shadr was there, the force of her inside Nerra like a tidal wave, pushing aside everything else.

You cannot win. Your dragon is nothing.

They met in another searing pass of magic-filled breath, the air around them superheated by flame and then cooled by shadows. Nerra felt Alith dive and then rise again, obviously trying to get above Shadr. This high above the city, the air was filled with smoke and clouds, reducing visibility until even Nerra's enhanced eyes couldn't pick out their foe, while her nose was too filled with the scent of burning to pick them out that way.

I know where you are, Shadr assured her. *So does my rider. He can feel you.*

"And I can feel you," Nerra whispered. Did Shadr think that the connection between them only ran one way? She pointed. "She's there, Alith."

The blue dragon turned, barely avoiding Shadr as the dragon queen came past in the clouds, claws extended to rake and tear. Her own claws scraped down Shadr's side, but even though the impact was enough to shake Nerra in her place atop Alith's back, it wasn't enough to do more than send a shower of black scales down toward the ground like fallen roofing tiles.

For a minute or more, that was the fight: passing by one another in the clouds by feel, coming out of their lack of visibility, striking and wheeling away from one another again. Shadr and Alith both left small wounds upon each other, and Nerra found to her dismay that she could feel the pain from both sides. She was connected to Alith now, but there was still enough of a link left between her and Shadr for the pain to carry over. She winced with every blow, having to cling harder to Alith's back.

Around her, the clouds crackled with lightning, and Nerra couldn't tell if that was because of the energy Alith had spat at her foe, or because a greater storm was brewing. Either way, it jumped and popped around her, making Nerra's skin tingle with the threat of what might come. She hunted around, trying to find Shadr again, preparing herself for the next flashing clash.

You hunt for us the way I hunted your brother, Shadr whispered in her mind. *Except that I have a magus beside me. Let me show you what he can do.*

Nerra pointed Alith in the direction that she felt Shadr talking to her from, and her dragon wheeled, ready for another strike. They started forward, hoping that one more pass would do it, one more strike. Then the impossible happened:

Shadr simply disappeared from Nerra's mind.

It took Nerra a moment to realize what that had to mean, and when she did, her horror bled over toward Alith even before she managed to cry out the words:

"It's a trap, Alith!"

It was too late, because Shadr was already coming in from the side, and now there was no time to turn to face her. Nerra felt the bulk of the black dragon slam into Alith, like two giant boulders smashing into one another. That was almost enough to shake her free from Alith's back.

Worse, the impact brought her close to Shadr's new rider. He sat there with the determined look of someone who had been in too many battles, and even as Nerra watched, he lifted a hand toward her.

Force impacted with her, hitting Nerra with all the power of a hurricane, and Nerra had only the briefest of moments to recognize the magic for what it was before it sent her tumbling from Alith's back,

121

over and over in the open air. She saw Alith start to fall too, brought down by one of Shadr's strikes, bleeding from her side as she fell, trying to right herself in the air and failing.

Nerra found herself staring up toward Shadr as she tumbled. The great black dragon had her mouth open toward Alith, as if she might finish her off as she fell. Nerra knew that she was dead, knew that there was no way that she could survive this fall, but she could still do *this*.

"What's wrong?" Nerra demanded, throwing everything she could into any remnant of the connection there had been between them. "Afraid that she meant more to me than you?"

Shadr roared at that, and her head whipped round toward Nerra. *You are mine, not hers! Mine to command. Mine to* destroy*!*

"I was never yours," Nerra whispered, as that great maw opened, fire starting within its depths. She found herself thinking of Greave, who had stood up to Shadr with more bravery than anyone she'd known. She thought of her brothers and sisters, and of her parents; all the people she had been connected to by love, not just some accident of magic. In the last moments before everything was flame and heat and death, she managed four simple words. The only ones that mattered.

"I am my own."

*

Devin hurt, but right now there was no time for him to hurt. It didn't matter that his body made him want to cry out in pain every time he took a step, not when the battle for the city was still continuing. He stumbled along the street, using one of the walls for support, heading in the direction of the castle. Lenore would be there, and Devin didn't know what to do now except get back to her and try to protect her.

Some of the smaller, lizard-like creatures had gotten into the city. One came at Devin, fast as a snake, but even hurt like he was, he was far from helpless. Using the pain to focus his mind, he sent out a blast of magic to set it off balance, then struck out with *Loss*, taking its head from its shoulders. A second came at him, and Devin cut that one down in a line from shoulder to hip. Then he was in clear space, still going toward the castle. One of the bridges lay ahead.

A dragon came tumbling down from the sky, bleeding from one side, impacting the ground hard enough to shatter stone and send up dust. Devin felt the ground under his feet shake with the impact, so that he was barely able to keep his footing.

Above, the great black dragon Anders rode hung there in the sky, flames targeting a smaller figure that seemed to hang in midair with their force, before tumbling down to strike the waters of the river below, quickly lost in them. The dragon started to swing toward Devin, or at least toward the dragon that had landed so close to him.

Devin knew that he ought to run. If Anders and his dragon spotted him, then Devin would quickly find himself having to dodge dragon fire, trying to fight back alone against both his enemy and the creature Anders rode.

Only he wasn't alone. Devin had thought that the dragon in front of him must be dead, that nothing could survive a fall like that. He'd thought of Memnir's deadly impact with the ground, and assumed that this was one more huge body filling the streets of Royalsport, never to move again.

Instead, one golden eye opened and stared at him with all the intelligence and power of its kind. Even as the black dragon above started to come down lower, looking to finish the job, it started to raise its head.

Devin found himself stepping forward then, putting a hand on the creature's flank. He *knew* how to do this now. Joining with Memnir had shown Devin what it took to connect with one of dragon-kind. More than that, he recognized this dragon. He knew it, because he'd been faced by it before. It was the dragon Devin had released from the cave, back in the forest what seemed like a lifetime ago. In that instant, he understood; he was *exactly* where he needed to be. He'd been through so much, but without it, he would never have learned to control his magic. If Master Grey hadn't sent him after Memnir, then he would never have learned what he needed to be able to do *this*.

Connection, instant and total. In that moment, Devin was Alith, and the dragon was him. He knew this dragon's every thought, knew its instincts and its needs. The connection was even deeper than it had been with Memnir. Devin understood more then, could *do* more. He opened himself to the magic coursing through him, and used it to help repair the dragon's wings. Devin and Alith stared upward in concert, looking at the dragon who hung over them ready to strike.

Devin had been trained to see, trained to look at the world in ways that only a sorcerer could look. He saw Shadr hovering there on mighty

123

wings, and he saw the weakness, saw the moment in between wingbeats when she would be vulnerable. Through his eyes, he knew that Alith saw it too.

She took to the air in a surge of violence, heading toward the queen of the dragons like a dart made of scales and claws. She flew up with all the speed of the lightning that poured from her mouth, making Shadr rear back, and as she did so, Alith's jaws clamped down on the softer scales of her underbelly, tearing through them and pulling back to reveal a heart larger than Devin beneath. Those jaws clamped down on it, and Shadr cried out, dying.

Alith pulled back from her, throwing her away from her tearing jaws. Shadr seemed to hang there for a moment, before falling from the sky, still wings no longer able to support her. Devin saw Anders fall from her back as she tumbled, twisting in midair, but managing to catch onto the edge of a building as he fell. He pulled himself up to safety even as Shadr fell past him.

The queen of the dragons slammed into the ground, rubble and dust rising as she fell. She twitched once, and lay still. Above, dragons shrieked in pain and confusion as their queen died. Those who followed her milled in confusion, clearly not understanding what they were meant to do next.

Perhaps if things had been different, that might have been the end of it, but Devin knew that this wasn't ended, not yet. Anders was still there, clambering to safety on the rooftop, the amulet around his neck as he looked up to call to the dragons. Devin knew that he couldn't give him any chance to do that. He had to stop him, and that was fine by him, after everything Anders had done.

Drawing *Loss*, Devin started to clamber up onto the rooftop after him. This ended, now.

CHAPTER TWENTY FOUR

Anders picked his way along the roof, looking down at the fallen form of Shadr, which filled one of the nearby streets, rendering it all but impassable. He found that he felt nothing at that loss, only a kind of emptiness where the creature's presence had once been.

The dynamism and power of the dragon was gone in death, and so too was the cruelty, the need to destroy. Anders had underestimated just how much of that would come back along the connection he'd forged through the amulet. Anders didn't mourn the loss of a creature that would have killed him if he'd shown a moment of weakness.

Perhaps another man might have thought that the battle was over for him, too, after the loss of such a powerful ally. He wasn't going to stop, though, not now. Shadr had given Anders an easy way to control the rest of the dragons, but he still had the amulet, and there were plenty more dragons left in the sky. Besides, Devin wasn't dead yet.

That mattered to Anders almost more than the rest of it, so that he hurried down the stairs leading to ground level, determined to reach his foe. He stepped out onto the cobbles of the street, and Devin was there at the far end, waiting for him. The arrogance of that, thinking that he could stand against Anders, even now.

"You should have stayed in the fissure I pushed you into," Anders called out.

"Why, Anders?" Devin called back. "Why do it at all?"

Anders laughed at that. "Do you really believe that nonsense Master Grey spouted about us both having a part to play in all this? There's only room for *one* Chosen One here, and I'm him."

"A boy out of destiny who brought dragons down on them," Devin countered. "You're a traitor to the kingdom. How many people have died today, when you could have stopped it?"

"Do you think anyone will care once I stop the attack?" Anders asked. "Do you think anyone will *know*? I'll use the amulet to bring the dragons to heel and be a hero. I'll have anything I want. I'll take the queen for my wife, and rule here as a king."

"People know what you are," Devin said. Devin had *Loss* in his hands now.

"What?" Anders shot back. He took a step toward Devin. "I was betrayed at every turn. I gave my whole life to this. Once I kill you, no one will know anything other than what I *tell* them."

Anders could picture it now. He could use the amulet to control the dragons, on *both* sides, and claim that he was the one who had stopped all of this, rather than bringing it to their doors. The people would give him anything, and if they didn't, well, with an army of dragons, he could simply *take* it.

"You're wrong about one thing though," Devin said. "This moment did need both of us. Without you, I wouldn't have reached Memnir and learned to connect to dragons. Without you, they wouldn't be here, now, in this moment. We've both done so many things, and without every single one of them, we wouldn't be in this place, ready to change everything."

"Now you just sound like Master Grey," Anders said. He took out the amulet. "Let me show you what *real* magic is about."

He raised the amulet to the sky, concentrating on it. With so many dragons up above, the sheer number of them was a little overwhelming. The temptation was to try to latch onto all off them; to command them all in a great flock of scaled beasts. The power that would take was immense, though. For now, he only needed one. His eyes latched onto the one that Devin had used to kill the dragon queen, still circling as if it might strike down. That one would do nicely. Let Devin be slaughtered by his own creature, and then Anders would take everything. He focused his will through the amulet, reaching out for the creature.

That was when a large, red-haired man ran past and snatched the amulet from his hands.

*

The art of being a good thief was the art of waiting for the perfect moment. The art of being a *great* one was recognizing that moment when it came. Renard was, by any definition, a great thief.

It had taken considerable patience to get into position to do anything in a fight like this. So much that, to the unpracticed eye, it had

126

probably looked like he was cowering away in the shadows, waiting for the violence above him to abate enough to run to safety.

And maybe there had been a little of that, if he broke the habit of a lifetime and tried being honest with himself. After all, he'd done his part. He'd traveled from one end of the kingdom to the other. He'd stolen the amulet, faced down the Hidden, or at least run away from them, been on a quest for the kingdom's sorcerer, ridden a dragon.

He'd fallen off that dragon too, and that one had hurt, even if Renard had a lot of practice by now at rolling when he fell. Without a dragon to aid in the fight, there hadn't been a lot he could do, so he'd found a spot where he could watch the action unfold and wait for his moment.

Now it had come, and he had seized it. No one was more surprised than Renard.

"Die!" the young man who had to be Anders shouted after him, and Renard ducked on instinct. A section of wall in front of him burst apart as if it were made from sand. Renard threw himself to the side, and another blast of magic went past him.

Renard should probably have been used to this kind of thing by now. In the last few weeks, he'd dodged everything from magic to dragon's breath, but that didn't stop his heart from pounding in his chest with the fear of it, or his eyes darting around for the next place to dodge to. He rounded a corner just ahead of another burst of power and kept moving.

Above, the battle continued. Dragons tore at one another, and Renard had a moment of terror as one swooped down too close. He didn't stop his sprint though. This wasn't the moment to pause.

There was an art to running away, and it was one most people didn't practice. They thought that it was enough just to be fast, or worse, they thought that fear would *give* them that speed, as if fear weren't a bigger thief than Renard was. A man like him had never been able to rely on that, so he'd had to learn the skills of it instead: when to dodge and when to put in bursts of speed, which obstacles he could fling himself over and which would slow him down too much, when to fight and when to hide.

Renard leapt over a low wall, ducked under a line for hanging clothes, and kept going. He could feel the amulet starting to chip away at his strength, slowly taking more of his life force as its curse took hold. Renard ignored it. With the time the curse would take to kill him he would be *grateful* if he lived that long right now. Rounding a corner to break Anders's line of sight, Renard ducked into cover and waited.

There was a time to run, and there was a time to hide. When a foe could strike at you from a distance, merely keeping that distance didn't help. Instead, Renard ducked into the space between a building and the wall that marked the edge of the property that went with it, using it to hide himself from Anders's sight. Above, dragons screeched and roared as they fought. He heard the sound of Anders's feet running past, but then they stopped.

"Do you think I can't *feel* the amulet, thief?" he called out. "Come out, give it back to me, and at least I'll make your end a swift one."

Why did people always think that was such a good thing? More time was always better, because at least then there was a chance to think of something *else* that would put death off a little longer. Renard eyed the wall beside him, spotting the missing bricks there that might conceivably serve as footholds. He would have to be desperate, though, to try something so exposed.

As the bricks beside him shattered under the impact of another of Anders's spells, Renard decided that he was *exactly* desperate enough to try it. He flung himself at the wall and climbed faster than he'd ever climbed before. A word from Anders and the wall twisted like a living thing to try to throw him off, but Renard was already flinging himself onto the roof beyond. He scrambled and dodged, making sure that he didn't stay still even for a moment. Renard leapt from roof to roof, and when the tiles gave way beneath his feet, he was moving so fast that there wasn't even time to fall.

"There's nowhere for you to run, thief!" Anders called out behind him.

That, of course, was the final part when it came to running away. The point was to have somewhere to run to. If all you could do was keep running, then that meant eventually, you ran out of road. The trick was to find safety before that point, but where could possibly be safe *here*?

Only one place.

Renard ran across the next rooftop at breakneck speed, flung himself from the edge, and hung there in the air for a moment before he landed hard. He tried to roll, but that was one of those tricks that was easier in theory than practice, and in any case only took *some* of the impact out of it all. He groaned as he rolled to a stop, then sat up as

Anders dropped lightly down behind him. The body of Shadr lay just a little way away, because Renard had been running back along the path they'd taken, only high above.

"All that just to run in a circle, thief?" Anders said. He raised his hands, ready to strike at Renard, and Renard managed a smile.

"There is one good thing about circles," Renard said as Anders started to prepare his spell. "If there's someone waiting behind who needs time to prepare, a big enough one can give him all the time he needs."

Devin's spell slammed into Anders from the side then, sending him sprawling. Anders came up, drawing a sword ready to fight, but Devin already had his own blade out. The two of them faced off against one another, and Renard could feel the air starting to crackle with magic.

"You can't beat me," Anders said. "You've never been able to beat me."

"We'll see," Devin said. He took his sword back in preparation for his first blow. "Time for this to end."

CHAPTER TWENTY FIVE

Devin swung *Loss* at Anders, and the other boy jumped back, swinging his own blade in return. Devin hoped that his sword would simply cut through the one Anders held, but Anders managed to change the angle of the impact, deflecting it rather than meeting the edge of the blade head on.

Anders threw a blast of magic, obviously expecting an easy victory that way now that Devin didn't have Sigil to focus his power through. Devin raised a hand and deflected it anyway, sending the power skidding off into a nearby building so that bricks shattered and fell.

"How?" Anders said, stepping back and winding up for another spell.

"I'm not who I used to be," Devin said. "I've seen more. I know how to look now."

He saw the air around them, saw the way the small currents of it ebbed and flowed. Before, he might only have been able to do this in the depths of his connection to Sigil, or when he'd been driven to the brink of death. Now, it was simple. He reached out and shifted those eddies until they lined up, forming a sudden blast of wind that knocked Anders sideways.

"No, it's not possible," Anders said. "You're nothing. You haven't had any of the training I have!"

He lunged at Devin, obviously trying to catch him off guard, but Devin slid away from the blow, kicking at his knee so that he stumbled away.

Devin started toward him, but had to throw himself to one side as sudden flames licked the ground from above, hot enough that it was like standing next to one of the furnaces in the House of Weapons. Devin looked up to see a dragon passing overhead, only for another to slam into it from the side.

It seemed that even after Shadr's death, the battle for the sky was continuing, dragons wheeling and blasting one another with their deadly breaths, unwilling to give up the fight. For a moment, as the flames licked close to him, Devin could only stare at the enormity of it.

He'd opened his mind to the patterns of the world, and now he saw them in every hint of magic the dragons used, in everything that they were.

That was the moment that Anders struck, lunging forward with his blade. Devin twisted aside a little, but even so, it pierced his side and came out again, leaving agony in its wake.

"Devin!" Renard called, but the thief was in no position to help. The flames of the dragon's blast were between Renard and the two of them.

Besides, this wasn't Renard's fight. This was about him and Anders.

"Go," Devin said. "Do what you have to do."

The thief took off running, and when Anders moved to find a way to follow, Devin stepped into his path.

"We aren't done," he said, raising *Loss* again.

"You can't beat me," Anders replied. "I don't care how much you think you've learned, you're still just a boy with a blade you're not worthy of, trying to live up to a destiny that was never yours."

He struck out again, and this time Devin managed to parry the blow, but his injuries made it harder to strike back. Anders was able to slip aside from the blow, and then they both had to duck as a fresh blast of dragon fire sent up a cloud of stone fragments and smoke from a building near them.

Anders gave ground and Devin followed, the two of them trading sword blows. There was no doubt that Anders was the better swordsman and Devin's injuries slowed him, but the power Devin had built into *Loss* made up for it, fueled by all the pain Devin felt.

He couldn't look at Anders without seeing the moment that the other boy had thrust a blade through Sigil's heart, slaying the wolf simply because of the connection it had with Devin. It was more than that, though. So many people he'd known were gone now, dead or lost thanks to the wars that had rocked the kingdom. The pain of that hummed in time with the emotions that he'd put into the sword's making, and the power within the weapon meant that he could match Anders stroke for stroke.

Their weapons clattered from one another in jarring blows, and Anders still gave ground, clearly not trusting his sword to hold against a direct blow from the sword Devin had crafted. He used the space he

131

gained to throw magic at Devin, first casting razor shards at him, then a burst of crushing force.

Devin saw how the first was made, unraveling the weaving even as it came at him. With the second, he whispered the air before him into a shield, deflecting the blow so that it rang like a hammer against an anvil.

Devin grasped the strands of smoke coming from one of the nearby fires, turning them into a strangling rope that sought Anders's neck. Anders whispered a word, so that the edge of his blade shone with light, and he cut through the spell the way he might have with an ordinary rope.

They came to an open space and circled one another, while above the dragons continued their fight. The roars and hisses of the violence above were so loud that Devin could barely hear his own breathing, even though he was panting with the effort of the violence.

"Getting tired?" Anders asked.

"Aren't you tired of it?" Devin asked. "Aren't you tired of all the death, all the violence?"

"It will be over just as soon as I kill you," Anders said. Devin knew that wasn't true, though. If Anders won here, it would never stop. He would want his place running things. He would slaughter anyone who didn't agree with him.

Including Lenore.

That thought forced Devin forward, swinging attack after attack at Anders. His opponent deflected and dodged, never standing still, never giving Devin a target that would let him finish this. He thought he saw an opening to thrust *Loss* through, but Anders twisted aside from it, stepped back, and whispered something.

It was like a blanket had fallen over Devin. He felt the power coming from *Loss* fade in his hands, and felt the magic around him as if it were trapped behind a pane of glass. Anders wasn't throwing magic at him in that instant, though, and that suggested that the connection to magic was gone for him as well.

"You think you're strong with your tricks," Anders said. "But when I take that away, you're *nothing*, and I am still everything I trained to be."

He attacked Devin then, and Devin understood in that moment just how much *Loss* had been making up for the difference in skill between them. He'd learned his lessons watching the masters at the House of

132

Weapons, but Anders had been given real lessons by sword masters, and it showed. Devin had to parry blow after blow, and not all of those parries were good enough.

He felt pain as wounds opened on his arms, his shoulders, his chest. He managed to stop any getting through too deeply, but still, each cut that Anders managed to open was one more to leach away his lifeblood.

"You've accomplished only one thing in your life," Anders said. "And you're holding it. When you're dead, I'll take that sword and tell the queen that you passed it to me as you died. Do you think she'll be grateful, Devin?"

Devin roared and threw himself forward, only for Anders to move out of his path and throw him expertly to the floor. He tried to stand, but Anders let his blocking spell fall and threw another blast of magic in almost the same instant. It slammed into Devin, sending him flying.

For a moment, everything went black. When Devin recovered his wits, the other boy was standing over him with his sword held in two hands, ready to thrust it down through Devin's heart. Devin tried to bring *Loss* up to block the blow, but it was no longer in his hand. Instead, it lay several paces away, waiting for Anders to claim it when he'd killed Devin.

Devin couldn't do anything then except look up past the other boy, staring at the ways the dragons above banked and soared, fought and blew blasts of flame at one another. He stared at those fights, thinking of the first time he'd tried to light a fire with magic, and how he'd almost killed himself doing it. Now he was going to die anyway, here, on the cobbles of Royalsport's streets. It didn't seem right, somehow.

In that moment, Devin saw it. He *knew* how they did it. He still had the link between him and Alith. Maybe the knowledge came through that link, or maybe it was simply so obvious that he should have cursed himself for not understanding it all at once. There was a reason all dragons could breathe fire, and there was a reason it was their breath.

"Anders," he said. "Master Grey once told me that I should never try to start a fire with raw magic."

"Are you trying to distract me with stories of the old fool?" Anders said. "He knew nothing, and taught me less."

"He taught you everything. You just didn't see it," Devin said, and reached for the magic he could feel.

The secret to the fire the dragons breathed was simpler than Devin could have thought. Any magus who understood balance knew how

133

much the order of the world longed to break into chaos. You couldn't force them into being, couldn't fuel them with the life in a body, but to free them, to simply *let* them be... you just had to be willing to burn with it. That was so simple that the youngest of the dragons could do it. All it took was a breath.

Devin blew gently in Anders's direction, waved a hand, and Anders's clothes burst into flames, all at once. Agony burst within Devin's skull, but he held to it as Anders became covered by the flames, screaming and stumbling away from Devin as he did so, like a torch that had been dipped in pitch. The pain in Devin's skull only increased. Maybe on another day, Devin couldn't have done this, but here, now, it was harder to *stop* the flames from coming than to bring them into being.

He stood, although the wounds Anders had inflicted on him made that so much harder than it should have been. He went to *Loss* and lifted it, feeling the power of the blade once again.

He struck with the sword, bringing it around in a single, sweeping arc that met Anders's neck halfway. His enemy's still burning form tumbled in that moment, his head bouncing away onto the cobbles.

Devin let the magic fall, the pain of it ebbing from him. He stumbled, stood, and finally leaned against a half ruined wall, trying to make sense of his victory. The power that had flowed through him was more than anything he could have believed, and after so long Anders was dead. Devin felt a brief pang of regret at that, because he knew Anders hadn't started as anyone evil. He'd just lost too much.

Devin had, too. He wanted to believe that it was done, that it was finally over.

The only problem was that the dragons were still fighting overhead. The battle wasn't done yet.

CHAPTER TWENTY SIX

Renard moved through the city at speed, not waiting to see how the fight with Devin and Anders went. If anything, he needed to put as much distance as possible between him and that fight, so that if it went the wrong way, Anders wouldn't be able to come after him and cut him down.

Fear propelled him, but also the sense that this... well, this was what he *needed* to do. No, it was worse than that. This was what he was *meant* to do. Him as a hero; oh, the gods must be laughing right now.

He used the rooftops to travel as much as possible. Partly, it was because that gave him a better view of the violence still taking place overhead, letting him see the flames of the dragons as the great creatures still clashed in the skies above Royalsport. They soared and dove, clawed and bit, raked one another with blasts of fire and occasionally dropped down to strike at the city with the same deadly power.

Staying on the rooftops where he could see them coming meant that when a blast of fire struck a building in front of him, Renard was able to fling himself sideways, jumping across an open space to impact on the tiles on the far side. Renard forced himself back to his feet and kept running.

The other thing about staying up on the roofs of the city was that at least it kept him away from the dangers that lay at street level. Renard could see the fires down there, people working in long lines to try to fight the worst of them.

There were other dangers too: gangs of the human-sized, lizard-like creatures had gotten into the city proper, so that now they fought on the streets with Royalsport's defenders. Some stupid instinct told Renard that he should jump down and join that fight, but that wasn't his fight, not now. He had the amulet. He had to make the most of this moment.

He looked around. Instinctively, he felt that he needed height for this. His eyes sought out the towers of the House of Scholars, but too many of those were burning, and the castle was too far away for this moment. He found his eyes drifting over to the silk-draped shell of the House of Sighs. Renard smiled tightly at that thought. Why not?

He skimmed from roof to roof like a thrown stone, heading for the heart of the entertainment district as flames burst around him, and Renard had to fling himself to the side again, but there was something indiscriminate about the strike. The dragons weren't targeting him, at least.

Only when he looked up, Renard saw one with its eyes locked firmly on him. It was a huge, blood red thing, with spines running down its back and horns sticking from its skull.

"Why did I have to go and think it?" Renard demanded aloud as he kept running. The dragon swooped in toward him, mouth opening to blast him with flame. Renard knew that there was no way he was going to be able to avoid this one, because the dragon could simply cover the whole roof he was on with flames if it wanted.

As a last resort, Renard held up the amulet, keeping it between him and the dragon. The creature hung there in the air, staring at him. It didn't strike, though, didn't use the deadliness of its breath. Renard could feel the power of the amulet reaching out to the dragon. The creature swooped over him and circled, still looking down at him.

Renard started to back away slowly, pace by pace, keeping the amulet between him and the dragon the way he might have a shield. He dared a glance over his shoulder, picking out the route he needed to take in order to make it to the House of Sighs. It wasn't far now, but to do it like this made it far harder.

He held the amulet over his head and ran for the door, dropping down to ground level, feeling the impact and keeping moving. Renard could see other dragons gathering overhead, staring down with all the fascination of cats looking at a mouse. Renard leapt over a fallen body, threw himself at the doors of the House of Sighs, and hammered at them.

"Let me in!"

The doors opened a crack, and Renard pushed his way in, ignoring the way the servant who answered the door drew a knife.

"Renard?" the young woman said. "Lady Meredith says—"

"There's no time," Renard said. "I need to get to the roof!"

He ran past, hoping that he wouldn't be stabbed in the back on the way. He hurried up the first set of stairs, looked around for the next set, and found himself face to face with Meredith.

136

She was bloodied and her dress was torn. She had bandages in one hand, which apparently she'd been using to patch up one of the people who had come into the House of Sighs for shelter. Even like that, she was beautiful enough that Renard stared.

"What are you doing back here?" she demanded.

"Trying to save everything," Renard said. "I think. I hope."

He heard Meredith sigh. "I suppose if I ask for details, you're going to tell me that there's no time, and I should just trust you?"

At that moment, an impact came against the walls of the building, making them shake, and bringing plaster falling down from the ceiling onto Renard's head. Stones fell from one part of the wall, letting a clawed hand reach through so that people had to throw themselves back to avoid it.

"That depends," Renard said. "How much time do you want to spend with dragons trying to get in here, to take this amulet?"

Meredith stared at him. "I should stab you just for bringing this kind of danger to my people."

"Or you could show me to the top of this place, and maybe I can *stop* this," Renard suggested.

Meredith took a suspiciously long time to make her mind up about that one. "Oh, very *well*. Follow me."

She led the way up through the building, and Renard followed as quickly as he could. Around them, the walls of the House of Sighs continued to shudder with the impact of dragons trying to get inside it. Renard just had to hope that he could reach a good spot to use the amulet before they peeled the whole place open like an orange.

The two of them went up through stairwell after stairwell, until Renard was far more out of breath with the climb than he should have been.

"Look at the great hero," Meredith said with a faint smile. "Barely able to stand up."

"I've run across half the city!" Renard insisted. It wasn't just that, though. Already, the amulet was having a small effect on him. It wasn't too bad yet, but it would only get worse. "How close are we?"

Meredith gestured to a door, unlocking it with a key from her belt. "That will lead to the roof. Then we can do... whatever it is you're going to do."

"We?" Renard said. He shook his head. "You need to stay here, Meredith. I wouldn't want to lose you."

137

"You don't *have* me, you oaf," Meredith said. "And if you think I'm going to let you out onto that roof alone, you're—"

Before she could finish, Renard leaned into kiss her. There was no time to do it properly, but at least it gave him a moment to snatch the key from her hand. He darted through the door, slammed it behind him, and locked it.

"Renard!" Meredith bellowed behind him in anger. Renard could already imagine her starting to work on the lock with picks and tools. It didn't matter; he'd done everything he could to keep her safe.

Renard was out on the roof of the House of Sighs, now, dizzyingly high above the ground. He came out into the open air to see dragons circling above, and now there were far more of them. Battles continued above the rest of the city, but here above the entertainment district, it seemed that every one of the dragons was wheeling around and around the House of Sighs, staring in at it with an intensity that made Renard want to flinch away.

He didn't, though. Instead, he lifted the amulet. He might not be the powerful magus the creator of the amulet had in mind to wield it, but that didn't make a difference right now. He was the one who was here, in the place that mattered. It probably fit with the rest of Renard's life that he was barely sneaking past the defenses of the amulet thanks to the quirks of his ancestry.

He lifted the amulet, feeling faintly stupid to be doing it when he didn't know how to use the powers within it. Renard tried to focus on the dragons around him.

He felt them then. Renard felt their presence like lead weights resting on the edges of his mind. He could feel their power, and the intensity of their magic, their strength and their hunger. The sheer number of them was awe inspiring, and a part of Renard wanted to shrink down away from them. Who was he to do this?

No, he wouldn't think like that. He was Renard. He'd stolen from the Hidden, from Lord Carrick, from Anders Samis. Renard forced himself to stand straight, and pushed out toward the dragons, reaching for them with a grasp that wasn't anything physical.

He felt the moment of connection like something clicking into place in his mind. In that moment, he wasn't one being, but hundreds of them. Renard wasn't one mind, but a whole constellation of them, pulling him in every direction at once.

138

Distantly, he could feel his body, and it hurt. He could feel the magic of the amulet, drawing at him, draining him, moment by moment. Renard did his best to ignore that, shouting out toward the dragons around him.

"Dragons, listen to me!"

Around him, the city fell suddenly silent. Renard realized then that it wasn't just the dragons around the House of Sighs that were staring at him then, but all of them. The ones that had fought for Anders, and the ones that had fought to stop them, all of them were hanging in the air on slow beating wings, or perched on the buildings of the city.

A single dragon flew down before him, and Renard recognized the deep, shining blue of its scales. This was the one that had killed the great black dragon Anders had ridden.

"It is time for the fighting to stop," Renard said. "You need to go. You need to leave the city."

Go where? The voice came into his head.

"Where did you come from?" Renard asked.

The city you call Astare, and before that, the continent you call Sarras.

"Then return there," Renard said. "Go back to Sarras."

The city is empty, and we seek a place near humans.

Renard tried to think. Could he just give away a city? Then again, if *anyone* could give away a place that wasn't his, it was probably him.

"You can have the city," he said. "It can be... like an embassy."

An embassy.

"A place where people come to talk," Renard explained.

Yes. There will need to be much talking.

"But not now," Renard said. "Now, you all need to go."

He gathered together all the strength that he could find. He threw it out at the dragons, pushing it through the amulet that he held. He yelled out a single word, which seemed to echo over the city.

"Go!"

Renard felt the power ripple out, and the dragons flew from the buildings like a flock of startled birds. They filled the sky, and this time they weren't fighting, they were fleeing.

He'd done that.

Renard felt himself collapse with the energy he'd put through the amulet, but he didn't care. He'd done it, he'd saved the city. He

139

distantly had the sense of someone standing over him as he started to fade toward darkness.

"I did it," he whispered up to them. "I saved... everyone..."

CHAPTER TWENTY SEVEN

Aurelle fought her way through the city streets, bursting from a doorway, running at one of the Perfected and firing one of her precious bolts. It clipped them, and they fell, the transformation already starting to take hold.

Aurelle kept running, heading for the next piece of cover. She was slightly too slow as claws from one of the more bestial creatures clipped her leg. Aurelle turned toward the creature, stabbing with a short knife. There was no time to kill the creature, but at least the strike made it rear back and gave Aurelle time to get into cover.

She pulled herself up over a wall and kept moving. It was important not to stop. She just had to trust that as the effects of Greave's cure took hold, the changing lizard creature would send its kin back away from the city. The ones before had.

There had been four before this one, each one approached in silence, and shot when Aurelle thought that there was the best chance of doing it without being caught up in a fight. She'd made her way through Royalsport like a ghost, and where she'd gone, the more human of the lizard-creatures had changed back into the people they'd been.

Five times now she'd done it, and each one had brought her far too close to dying. Aurelle had wounds on her now from claws and from weapons, so that her gray clothing was darkened with blood. She had scorch marks on her too, from where she'd gotten too close to dragon fire, and her hair was singed with it.

She knew that she looked ragged and beaten now, but she kept going, heading up toward the castle. Above, the dragons fought, and even if they were busier attacking one another than the city below, each blast of dragon fire still caused ruin there. Buildings crackled with flames, or fell apart under the impact of strikes by the dragons. Even when they died, the dragons caused destruction, their huge forms plummeting down onto houses and workshops.

Aurelle moved quickly, skirting around the body of one of the fallen creatures. It still twitched, one eye open and staring at her.

Aurelle thought about thrusting a dagger deep into that eye to end its life, but thinking of that brought back thoughts of Nerra. She walked on instead, leaving the creature to live or fade into death without her intervention.

Ahead, over the next of the city's bridges, Aurelle saw people fighting fires in some of the houses of the noble district. Servants stood beside nobles in the chain, throwing water over a burning house in an effort to quench the flames and stop its destruction. Aurelle hurried over in their direction, although she had her own task in all this chaos, and knew that she couldn't stop to help.

Greave was counting on her.

She crossed over into the noble district, and that was when she saw the force of the humanoid lizard things advancing on the people trying to save their homes. Aurelle cursed and tried to fit the last of her bolts to her crossbow.

"Run!" she yelled to the nobles and their servants. She had no reason to love nobles by this point, but the more people she could save, the better. "Run while you can!"

She tried to identify the more human one leading this pack of the creatures. She found it in the midst of them, walking among them the way a hunter might walk among a pack of dogs. Aurelle lifted her small crossbow and fired, straight for the creature.

The bolt struck one of the less humanoid ones instead. It shrieked like a wounded animal and fell to the floor, convulsing. To Aurelle's shock, the awful, twisted planes of its body started to correct themselves, turning to something more human, the flesh turning from scales to skin, the head starting to sprout the beginnings of hair. Her bolt worked on *these* foes, too, it seemed.

The only problem was that this one wasn't one of the leaders. It had no power to send away its fellows as it changed. Worse, the others around it seemed to sense the change in it, and even as a young woman stood up from among them, the other creatures fell on her, tearing her limb from limb while her cries of agony echoed.

If the nobles and their servants hadn't been running before, they did so now. Aurelle ran with them, then turned and threw a dagger at the leader of the pack of lizard creatures. This time it clipped the creature's arm, but without Greave's cure on the edge, it did nothing but encourage the whole pack to chase Aurelle.

142

That was good in one way, because at least it meant that Aurelle could lead the chasing pack down a series of alleys, away from the people they would otherwise have torn limb from limb.

The only problem was that without any more of the arrows, there was nothing she could do to stop the creatures from tearing *her* limb from limb too. Aurelle could only run, heading down another alley...

She cried out in frustration as it turned out to be a dead end. She took out the vial with the cure, took out a bolt, and stopped. If she did that, there would be none left to hand to the House of Scholars. She would change this foe, but every other one of the lizard folk would be stuck as they were. Greave's legacy would be gone.

Aurelle knew that she couldn't do that, so she took the vial and found a nook in the wall, hiding it. She stood by it, drawing her daggers. The most she could hope now was that her body would provide a marker to let people find the vial. She stood there, watching the dragons that swooped over the city as the creatures rounded the corner.

She looked away from them and got ready to throw herself forward. If she was going to die, it had to mean something. She would take as many of them with her as she could.

"I'll be with you soon, Greave," she whispered.

Then the lizard creatures stopped. They stood there, and then they turned and ran. Aurelle looked up, not understanding, at least until she saw the dragons turning and flying from the city, wingbeats carrying them away as swiftly as they'd come.

Aurelle didn't know what was happening, but she fell to her knees with relief all the same. It took an effort to clamber back to her feet. She wasn't done yet. She still had a promise to fulfill. Taking the vial she'd hidden, Aurelle tucked it away and set off for the castle once more.

In the streets around her, she saw people coming out of houses to stare at the retreating dragons. They stood there in silence, apparently not knowing what to do while the flames from the fires the dragons had started continued to lick at buildings.

"Don't just stand there," Aurelle shouted at them. "Fetch water to put the fires out."

She shocked them into movement with the suddenness of it, but Aurelle couldn't stop to help. Instead, she kept going toward the castle.

143

Now there were people moving through the streets, a few celebrating, others carrying the wounded or dead. Aurelle walked past them all, feeling numb now, and tired. Her wounds hurt, but she didn't dare stop to rest them.

When she reached the castle, the gates were in the process of opening, a pair of guards pushing them into place now that the dragon attack was done. Aurelle strode past them, or tried to. One went to challenge her, reaching for a sword.

"Do I *look* like a dragon to you?" she said, and didn't give them a chance to think before she shot her next question at them. "Where is the queen?"

She didn't need them to answer, though, because Aurelle could see the way the doors of the great hall had been blown open by some force Aurelle couldn't guess at. Had a dragon struck here?

Aurelle was running before she even thought about it, ignoring the shouts of the guards. She ran to the great hall and ducked inside, staring in horror at the destruction she found there. Rubble littered the floor, and beams had fallen haphazardly across the space there.

Lenore sat there among it, perched on a piece of rubble as large as the throne, somehow managing to make the rubble of the destroyed room seem just as elegant when she sat on it. Servants were rushing around her now, obviously bringing news of the events in the city.

Lenore looked up as Aurelle approached. "Aurelle? I'm so glad to see you alive."

"And I you, my queen," Aurelle said, relief flooding through her.

"Tell me, do *you* know what is happening in my city?"

Aurelle shook her head. "Only that the dragons are gone. I saw them leave in the moments before I came here. People are starting to deal with the damage."

"They will have all the help they need," Lenore promised. She started to turn to her servants to give commands. Aurelle knew that she should let her, that this was about all the people of the city. Still, she had to say something.

"There's more," Aurelle said. She couldn't keep the pain she felt at Greave's loss out of her voice. "There... there's something I have to tell you."

Lenore turned at that, and her expression said that she had an idea of what might be coming. She'd been the one to send Aurelle after Greave, after all.

144

"Where is Greave?" Lenore asked. "Did you manage to find him?"

Aurelle shook her head. She felt tears spring to her eyes. She'd held back the pain this long, thought about anything but this while she'd fought her way through the city. Now, she had to come out and say it.

"He… he's dead."

"Are you sure?" Lenore asked.

Aurelle nodded. "Your sister… Nerra, I met her. She told me that the dragon queen killed him."

"Oh, Aurelle, I'm so sorry."

Aurelle shook her head. She couldn't take sympathy, not now.

"There's more," Aurelle said.

"I'm not sure that I can take more," Lenore said, with a wince.

"This part is good," Aurelle said. She took out the vial that she had almost defended with her life. "This… your brother succeeded. He found a cure for the scale sickness. It can turn back the creatures the dragons transformed."

Lenore stared at Aurelle with obvious astonishment. "You're sure this works?"

Aurelle nodded. "I've tried it. I've seen it change them. I need the House of Scholars to work out what's in it."

"I'll have them analyze it," Lenore promised. "If we can get the ones like my sister back, then this will change everything. You've done more than you know, Aurelle."

"Greave did it," Aurelle said. "I just want the world to know about what he did."

"It will," Lenore promised. "And it will know all you've done too. Name a reward, and it is yours."

Aurelle shook her head. The one thing she wanted was something that no one else could help her with.

"May I leave, my queen?" she asked. She had fulfilled Nerra's request, and brought Greave's cure to the world. Now, she just felt empty. She could go back to the cliff in peace.

"No." To her surprise, Lenore put a hand on her shoulder. "No, I do not permit it."

"But, my queen—"

To Aurelle's shock, Lenore hugged her then, holding onto her while Aurelle cried, while they both did. Aurelle wept for what felt like an age, sagging down to sit on one of the pieces of rubble, her wounds finally catching up with her.

Lenore pulled back from her, looking her in the eye. "You are not alone here, Aurelle, and you do not get to be done. My brother would not want that."

"I..." Aurelle could only shake her head. "No, he wouldn't."

"I have a kingdom to rebuild, and I need my friends beside me," Lenore said. "Will you help me with that rebuilding?"

Aurelle paused. The pain was still there, but she pushed it back. For so long, she'd been the person others used to tear apart lives. Now, maybe, she would be able to build one. She suspected that it was what Greave would have wanted.

"Yes, my queen."

CHAPTER TWENTY EIGHT

Nicholas led the way back through Sandport, past the gates, down through the sand-filled streets. He leaned on Erin as he walked, but tried not to make it too obvious. Sandport was not a place whose leaders could afford to appear weak.

His men were spreading out, securing things, making the city safe again in the aftermath of the battle. The truth was that there were far too many factions in Sandport that would probably try to take advantage of a moment like this, but for now, everything seemed to be in order.

He could see Erin looking around at it, using her spear like a walking cane as she took in the sand on the streets, the vast space of the market and the districts centered around the wells. Around them, people came and went, each with a request or urgent news. Nicholas did his best to make sure that each went away feeling that everything was normal.

Ankari came up to them. "I have news. Ferrent fell in the battle."

That was a moment of pain in Nicholas's heart. Ferrent had been one of the last links to his father, and now he was gone. He'd died doing the thing he'd sworn to do, though: protecting Nicholas and the city.

"See that he is buried with honor," Nicholas said. He managed to keep the pain off his face, but only barely.

Ankari nodded. "Absolutely."

She went to do it.

"You seem hurt," Erin said. She was watching him carefully.

"One of my closest advisors is dead. He was... he was a friend. *Shouldn't* I be hurt?"

Nicholas kept walking with her, heading for the tower he ruled from.

"I've lost friends too, in this," Erin said. "All to try to stop a monster. And now I find that you're not a monster at all."

"Are you sure?" Nicholas asked.

Erin shrugged. "I'm pretty sure."

147

"And I'm pretty sure you don't plan to invade my country," Nicholas said. "And if you say your sister isn't going to, then… I guess I'm going to have to take your word for it."

"But it means that all the people I brought here, the ones who died… it was for nothing," Erin said.

They reached the tower. The doors were open, revealing people waiting for Nicholas. He didn't feel up to it. He knew he had to be the king he claimed, but right then, he wanted to rest.

Erin seemed to sense that, pushing past the assorted attendants and giving them looks that made even the fiercest of them back away.

"Can't you see he's hurt? Fetch a physiker, and then ask him all the things you want to ask."

"Thank you," Nicholas said, as she helped him up the stairs. He considered whether he should say the next part. How well did he really know Erin yet? How much did he dare with her?

Enough, he dared enough.

"Your friends who died; it wasn't for nothing."

Erin stopped and stared at him. Nicholas could guess at the pain she felt, the effort she was making not to lash out in her pain. "And how many of them are still alive? Fewer than half. Are *those* even alive?"

"I'll find out," Nicholas said. He turned and called back. "Find the ones from the Northern Kingdom. Have them come to my chambers. I have much to be grateful to them for."

"Like what?" Erin asked.

"Without them, you would not have gotten this far," Nicholas said. "And if you hadn't, then I would probably have died in that last fight with Inedrin. You saved my life, and you helped to kill someone who genuinely *would* have gone on to become a new Ravin."

Erin didn't say anything for a while. She kept helping him up to his rooms instead. When they got there, Nicholas could see her staring at the marble of the receiving room, the carved couches and the latticework shutters over the windows. She looked at the opulent rugs on the floor and the gilding of the ornaments as if she didn't believe they existed.

"Were you expecting something more austere?" he asked. "A tent filled with nothing but cushions? A warrior's room, with only a cot and a sharpening stone?"

"Now you're mocking me," Erin said.

148

"I'm not sure I'd dare," Nicholas replied. He made his way over to a couch and slumped down in it and gestured to the space beside him. "Can I offer you wine?"

"It helps, knowing that I stopped someone like Inedrin," Erin said, ignoring his offer. "And I guess, if anyone has to rule here, you're a good choice." She sighed then. "I guess I should go home and tell Lenore I did what she asked. Assuming I can, and I'm not a prisoner here."

"If you truly want to go, I'll have space made for you on the next caravan heading north," Nicholas said. "But if I'm honest... I'd rather that caravan just took a letter. It would be good if you stayed."

"You like me that much?" Erin asked with a snort.

Nicholas dared a smile. "Maybe. But maybe I also think that there's more chance for peace between our countries if we actually *talk* to one another. Having you here would help with that."

"As what?" Erin said. She took a seat now beside him. "A hostage?"

"Maybe an ambassador," Nicholas countered. "Who could deny your skills in diplomacy?"

"I could still change my mind about not killing you, you know," Erin said.

Nicholas had an idea then. "Why not take the role of captain of the guard here?" he suggested. "I need a new captain with Ferrent gone. I've seen you fight, and you're more than worthy of it."

"Plus, having a northern princess on your side implies to all the other would-be rulers of the Southern Kingdom that you have the North's support," Erin said.

Nicholas spread his hands. "If it means less time fighting those who would try to slaughter my people, I'll use any trick I can find. Besides, this one has the added bonus of you having to work closely with me."

"That's a bonus?" Erin said.

Nicholas nodded. "Yes, I really think it is."

*

Erin wasn't sure what to say to Nicholas's offer. He wanted her to stay there, with him? He was offering her the chance to be the captain of his guards, to serve as a conduit between the South and the North?

Was he offering her *more* than that?

149

Erin found herself staring at him. They were close to one another on the couch, close enough that Erin could smell the sweat of the battle on Nicholas's skin. There was a part of her, she had to admit, that wondered what it would *taste* like. Still, she had to ask it.

"Is this because you're in love with me, or something stupid like that?" Erin asked. She thought for a moment. "I mean... it's okay if you are... I guess..."

"You think I'm the kind of man to fall in love with a woman because she's been his captive?" Nicholas replied in that joking tone Erin was starting to realize was mostly a way of shutting out the truth.

"No, but I imagine one headbutting you in the face might do it," Erin shot back. They both laughed at that, and somewhere in the middle of all that laughter, she darted forward to steal a kiss from him, quick and sharp as a raid into some foe's lands, gone again before he could react.

"I'm not saying that I'm somehow in love with you," Erin said. "That would be *stupid*. I'm not some blushing maiden who says yes to everything because some big strong man has led her around his kingdom in chains."

"I think technically it was ropes," Nicholas pointed out.

"Shut up."

"You know, I *am* the ruler of the Southern Kingdom," Nicholas said.

"Then shut up, your majesty." Erin tried to think some more. "I'm not saying yes to anything, you understand, not now. But I am saying maybe, in time, possibly."

"Maybe, in time, possibly," Nicholas echoed. "That's the most romantic thing anyone has ever said to me."

"Still able to stab you," Erin reminded him.

"And my *actual* proposal?" Nicholas asked. "Where do you stand on becoming my captain of guards?"

That was easier. Erin knew that she would never be happy in times of peace. It wasn't in her. Even Lenore had seen it, which was probably why she'd sent her south in the first place. If she went back north, she would have a lifetime of standing by her sister's side, doing... what exactly? Probably nothing, kept safe by the presence of Lenore's armies. Here, she could help Nicholas to secure the throne he wanted, make sure that he didn't turn into a new Ravin, *and* help to keep the

150

Northern Kingdom safe from any threat from its southern neighbor, all at once.

"I… I'll need to write to my sister," Erin said.

"Of course," Nicholas said. He hauled himself to his feet and went to a chest, where he took out paper and ink, along with a long peacock feather to serve as a quill.

Erin took both and set them on a desk, trying to work out what she needed to say.

Dear Lenore, she began. *So… I'm alive, and safe, and no one has captured me, although they kind of did for a bit.*

She sighed, because this letter wasn't going the way she'd expected that it would. Still, she kept going; the important thing was to get down what she actually felt.

I went south, and I heard about a man named Nicholas St. Geste who was trying to become the new Ravin. Only it wasn't like that. I think that he's a good man, and that he can unite the Southern Kingdom for the better. We killed another one, who was like another Ravin, and I think there are more out there.

I'm planning to help him deal with them and unite the whole of the kingdom. I think he's someone who can make the whole place more stable and… what does it mean when your heart seems to flutter when you look at someone? It sounds like a stupid thing, out of a bard's song.

So I'm going to stay here, at least for a while, if you can spare me. I love you, and if you ever need me, I'll be there. But for now, this is where I need to be. If you want to make peace with anyone from the Southern Kingdom, make it with us.

Your Loving Sister,

Erin

The words didn't seem like enough. There were all kinds of things that she wanted to say to Lenore, but couldn't.

"I'll see her again," Erin said to herself.

"You will," Nicholas said. "For one thing, I want you there the next time we do any trade negotiations with the Northern Kingdom."

"I'm not going to betray my sister," Erin said.

"I know," Nicholas replied, but in a tone that suggested he didn't, not really. Erin suspected that it was one more argument to add to the list. She looked forward to it. She was still thinking about that when a knock came at the door.

Her friends came in: Sarel and Nadir, Ulf, Yannis and Bertram. All of them had small wounds, and were filthy from their travels. Erin was so glad to see that they were alive. She got up and hugged each of them in turn, even though Nadir looked uncomfortable with it, and Ulf's grip practically crushed her.

"So, are we going home?" Sarel asked.

"You are," Erin said. She held out the letter. "I need you to take this to Lenore. It explains... well, everything."

Sarel took it, tucking it away in her clothes.

"My people will see that you make it safely to a ship," Nicholas said, "and I'll pay for a ship for you back to your kingdom."

"But you aren't coming?" Yannis said.

Erin shook her head. "I have things to do here."

She looked over at Nicholas, imagining some of the things that the future might hold for them. There would probably be battles; there *might* be more kisses. Erin wasn't sure which she was looking forward to more.

"I will be staying here," Nadir said. "Sarit has found a place for me by his tribe's fires."

"But the rest of you will go back?" Erin said. They nodded. "And you'll take my message?"

"We will," Ulf promised.

That was good. Erin wanted Lenore to know what was going on. She looked over at Nicholas. She wasn't sure what the future held, but for now... now it was starting to look good.

CHAPTER TWENTY NINE

Devin found Renard in the aftermath of it all, slumped down on top of the House of Sighs. He was still clutching the amulet, and his hair was graying, lines etched into his face.

"You've done it, Renard," Devin said. "You've sent them away."

Renard looked up at him. "But the dragons... I can feel them. I need..."

Devin reached out for the amulet. Renard tried to snatch it back, tried to cling to it even then, but Devin pulled it clear of his grasp. The thief was too weak to stop him right then. How much had it taken to rid the city of dragons? Devin wasn't sure he could have done as much. Anders certainly couldn't, or he would have controlled all those involved in the fight.

Devin held up the amulet. It was too dangerous. He needed to do something.

*

Devin stood down by the shoreline, looking out over the raging expanse of the Slate River. The Southern Kingdom was just visible in the distance, and from here, it was possible to see the men and women working to rebuild one of the bridges between the two lands from that side. The Northern Kingdom's own people were working on their side, so that in a month or two, the two halves might meet again.

Devin suspected that he might be able to help with that. The pure flash of understanding he'd had staring at the dragons was gone, but it was easier to see things as they were now. With the right practice, a magus might be able to make a bridge grow from one side to another.

Then again, the more work people had to do to reach one another, the more they would probably value that connection.

Devin could still remember the effort it had taken for him to connect with the dragons, all that it had cost. He took out the amulet, watching the shine of the sun from its jewels and its central scale. This made it so much easier, but it also turned that connection into something that was about control, not mutual respect.

The magus who had made it had left it as a way for humanity and dragons to keep the peace between them. Instead, Anders had used it as a way to gain power over them, and to use them as a weapon. The Hidden who had sought it wanted it for that power. As long as it was out in the world, there would be people looking for it, looking to use its power for their own ends.

Devin could feel that power as he held it. He could understand the temptation of it. What were his choices now? He could wear it, keep it, use it. The power of it would undoubtably be helpful in dealing with dragons. If they struck at the kingdom again...

No, he couldn't think like that. If he kept it, it would be a tool of coercion. It would be a barrier to good relations with the dragons, not a way to bring them about. At the same time, it would be a magnet for those who wanted power for themselves. They would come after Devin, and if he stayed in Royalsport, that would bring danger to all those around him.

What else then? He could hide it, the way Master Grey had, but everything that had happened showed the dangers of *that*. He could lock it away behind defenses, but that was as much an invitation as a protection. He could go away to the ends of the world, where no one would find him, but to do that... He glanced back behind him. He couldn't do that.

Which just left this. Devin hefted the amulet, feeling the weight of it, and the power. He brought his arm around, and he threw it, as hard as he could, out into the roaring currents of the Slate. The amulet soared like a skimmed stone, then plummeted toward the waves. It struck those waves, sending up spray, and then disappeared from sight. Even then, Devin watched the spot a moment longer, half-convinced that it would somehow find a way to rise from the waves again.

No, though, the Slate swallowed it, its currents and its span enough to take in even the most powerful of objects. By now, it would already be in the process of being carried away toward the sea. Maybe a hundred years from now, it would be found again, but any treasure hunter would have to find a way to reach the bottom of the ocean.

Devin sighed with relief, and turned back from the edge of the great river.

"It's done," he said.

"It looked hard to do," Lenore said. She was standing there a little way away, waiting as if she knew how much he would need someone after this. The fact that it was her meant so much to him.

"It's just… it took so much to get to this point," Devin said. "It cost so much."

He found himself grieving in that moment for the people who hadn't made it to this point. Master Grey had taught him so much, even if he had never said all that he knew. The people he'd called his parents were still gone, their home empty.

He found himself reaching down reflexively for Sigil, but the wolf was gone too. He found himself grieving for the presence of the creature that had been his only companion for so much of this. Devin could still feel the pain and the anger that had come when Anders had killed Sigil.

Devin even felt a flash of grief for Anders, and what he had become. The two of them had set out on this journey, both of them destined to play their part in all of this. Anders could so easily have become a hero, but instead, he'd become a killer and led the dragons down to try to destroy them.

Of course, in the grand scheme of things, that *had* been his role in this. Without him, would things have turned out as they did? Devin suspected that he would never know.

"I know," Lenore said. Of course she did. Of her siblings, Erin was the only one living, and *she* was down in the Southern Kingdom. Everyone had lost so much in this. Devin could feel a wave of sympathy for her pain. "There's going to be a lot of rebuilding to do after this."

"I'll help in any way I can," Devin promised her. Anything Lenore needed, he would do. He loved her, and even if he couldn't say that, he could show it. He could be there. He could support Lenore with anything she needed.

"There is one thing," Lenore said. "Master Grey is gone. He killed himself to stop the Hidden. A ruler needs a sorcerer."

"You're asking me to be the Queen's Magus?" Devin said. That took him a little by surprise, even though he probably should have expected it. "I don't feel like I know enough. Master Grey didn't really teach me anything, just sent me out into the world to do the things he needed."

155

Devin thought about those quests, first to find star metal, then to learn to work it, to find the fragments of the unfinished sword, and to find the amulet. On each, it felt as if he'd gotten closer to magic, learning more about it just through the act of doing it. He couldn't have imagined at the start being able to do any of the things that he could do now.

"If not you, who else could it be?" Lenore said. "You would have his tower and his library, anything you need."

Devin *wanted* to be able to live up to everything she wanted him to be. He guessed that he could always learn as he went along. He suspected that Master Grey had been doing so for most of his life. He offered Lenore a bow.

"I would be honored, my queen."

"I'm glad," Lenore said. "And not just because people are less likely to revolt when they think you have a sorcerer on your side. It will be good knowing that you're still there."

That made Devin's heart swell with pride, but also with a kind of hope. Maybe there was a chance. No, he didn't dare to hope, not after everything with the Dance of the Suitors. He'd heard the story of what she'd done to avoid being tied down by a husband. Devin didn't know whether to feel hope at that or despair.

Lenore looked back behind her. There were guards there, of course, because there was no way that the queen could possibly travel all the way to the coast alone. The Knights of the Spur were no more, but Lenore had Aurelle and Orianne with her, along with half a dozen guards.

"We should be getting back," Lenore said. "There are still so many things to do back in the city."

"I know," Devin said. He sighed. "I went by the House of Weapons. They're starting to put things back in order, but they don't have the weapon masters they used to. Too many of them died in the fighting."

"We'll have to hold contests to find new ones," Lenore said. "Perhaps my new sorcerer could produce a suitable prize to attract the best of them?"

Devin rested a hand on the hilt of *Loss*. He didn't have any more star metal, but maybe ordinary steel could be made to take some of the runes that he'd worked into the fabric of the swords he'd made?

"I can try," he said. Anything she asked him to do, he would attempt.

"After that, I need to find a replacement for the knights we've lost," Lenore said. "If Erin were here, I would ask her to do it, but as it is…"

Devin thought of all the time he'd spent wishing he could be a knight when he was younger.

"Give the job to the peasants who joined the fight," he suggested. "Some of them won't want to go back to working on the land after fighting so much. If you give the best of them a job as your new knights, it will stop them becoming bandits, and they'll be loyal to you rather than to whatever noble house they're from."

"The nobles won't like it," Lenore said.

"Your nobles will respect it," Devin said. "They'll see that you have a force that is all your own, and they'll be less likely to push at your laws. My guess is that in a few years, they'll be sending second sons to join them."

Lenore smiled at that. "You've only been my sorcerer for a couple of minutes, and already you're giving good advice. Although I think for the full effect, you're meant to be a bit more cryptic about it."

"I can try that," Devin said.

Lenore took a step back toward the waiting retinue. Devin almost let her go, almost just followed in silence. He knew how much she had in her life right now, from the complexities of her nobles to the need to focus on rebuilding. She didn't need him to say anything right then.

The words came out anyway, without him meaning to. "Marry me."

Lenore stopped, turning to face him.

"I know you arranged the whole end of the Dance of Suitors so that you wouldn't have to marry anyone," Devin said. "I know if you pick one person, that means a dozen other factions are disappointed. I know that I'm not noble, or able to give you a diplomatic alliance, or—"

"Yes," Lenore said, and it took Devin a moment to realize that was what she had said.

"Yes?" he repeated.

"Of course I will," Lenore said.

"You will?" Devin said. He hadn't thought that she would ever say a thing like that. He hadn't thought that she would ever be *able* to.

"There's nothing I want more," Lenore said. She stepped into Devin's arms, putting hers around his neck. "Maybe my new sorcerer can promise me that it will all turn out all right."

157

Devin shook his head. "That's one thing I can't do. But I can promise I'll be there, whatever happens."

"Good enough," Lenore said, and kissed him.

CHAPTER THIRTY

Renard hefted his tankard, and the people of the inn around him cheered. For once, it wasn't even because they thought he might be about to fall down drunk.

"To my generous friends!" he said, quaffing the ale he held.

Around him everyone else drank, and someone pressed another drink into his hand.

"Tell us the story again," the man said.

"*Again?*" Renard replied. Even he knew better than to tell the same story too many times in a row. "Are you sure you don't want the one about King Godwin the Second and—"

"No!" a young boy called out. "I want to hear *the* story!"

The others called out along with it, banging their tankards on the table, until it built into a cacophony of people demanding that he tell the whole thing again from the start. Renard didn't know what to do except oblige them.

"All right, all right," he said. "Settle down! So it all began in an inn much like this one, out on Lord Carrick's lands. That was where I first heard about the gold he'd stolen..."

Renard knew all the steps of the story by now; he'd told it enough times to know where people would laugh and where they would groan, where they would gasp in fear, and where they would look at one another with warmth.

He told them all of it, starting with the robbery and working up from there, through the arrival of the Hidden, them all but buying him from Lord Carrick with a favor, them forcing him to travel to the hidden temple. Renard paused there, because he knew that people enjoyed this most when he made them wait for this moment.

"That was when I found the amulet," Renard said. "Hidden behind a door that the dragon following me couldn't get through..."

In earlier versions of this story, Renard had made himself braver, made himself stand and fight the dragon rather than sneaking past it and running, climbing and dodging.

159

Now, though, he just told it as he remembered it. For some reason, they seemed to like that more, even the bits where he did something stupid. *Especially* the bits where he did something stupid. Maybe Renard should have minded about that, but for now, there was only the story.

There was crossing the kingdom as the amulet slowly drained him, the debacle at Geertsport, running into Aurelle, the killer who had lost her prince. When he recounted running into Master Grey, people leaned in closer. When Renard talked about that first fight with the Hidden, they gasped. He told them about losing the amulet and almost walking away from it all, and they assumed that it was just a natural step in the story of a hero.

They didn't know him at all.

Renard got through it: going back, being sent after Devin. When he talked about Memnir towering over them, it was like he was back there, certain again that he was going to die. When he talked about the final battle, the fire and the destruction, it was something everyone there could relate to.

"...and *that's* when I came in and snatched the amulet from the evil Anders's hand, running to get it away from him," Renard said. "I raced for high ground, and I..."

This was the part that he could never quite get right, because how could he describe being connected to every dragon, all at once? The words at this point always came out wrong, and in any case, people didn't seem to care.

"I made them turn and leave," Renard said. "I told them to go, and they went, to Astare, and to Sarras."

They cheered him, as they always cheered him, and more people offered to buy him drinks. A couple of the women leaned in to offer more than that, too. He was a hero again, beloved and believed. This time it probably wouldn't even fade. They'd *seen* the city saved, and enough people had seen him do it that Renard could probably live out the rest of his life as a hero, celebrated in story, feted wherever he went.

So why did he feel so empty?

The temptation was to fill the gap with beer, and praise, and possibly more beer after that. He could stagger from inn to inn, telling his story, and when his story was the story of everything that had happened with the dragons' invasion, there would always be an audience.

160

To his utter shock, though, Renard found that he didn't want to do any of that. People bought him drinks, and he left them on tables, pretended to sip at them. Beautiful women made suggestions that made even *him* blush, and he politely declined. Purses fell in easy reach, and he didn't even begin to steal from them. What was wrong with him?

Renard knew the answer to that: this wasn't where he wanted to be, and it wasn't *who* he wanted to be. Sure, he could do this for the rest of his life, but what would that look like? Him bloated and aging, telling the story of all he'd done until he died gout filled and drunk?

Once, that might have seemed like the kind of life he deserved, and a far better one than the noose he would probably earn from his thieving. Now, it didn't seem like enough. Now, he wanted to do... he shuddered at the thought... the *right* thing.

More than that, there was one thing he wanted to do more than anything else in the world.

*

Renard made his way through the city, and the strangest thing was the way people turned to stare at him as he did it. He suspected that he wouldn't be able to sneak in and burgle anywhere in a hurry.

He passed people trying to rebuild the city, putting their homes together and undoing the worst of the damage done by the dragons. It was going slowly, and Renard found himself wondering if he could have stopped some of that damage if he'd managed to get hold of the amulet earlier.

That was the problem with being a hero: whatever good he managed to do, there was always something better that he could have managed to do.

The strangest part was that the people who stared at him didn't see him as *him*. They never could. No matter how many times he told them the story, no matter how much effort he put into making sure that he didn't burnish what people thought of him, they still stared at him like he was a hero.

Renard didn't need that. He didn't need people looking at him like something he wasn't. He needed the one person who really saw him for what was.

He made his way through into the entertainment district, with the House of Sighs stretching out above him. Renard wasn't running this

161

ime, although a part of him wanted to. This couldn't wait. It was just hat, if he ran, half the city would probably run along in step with their lero. There was every chance that he would be crushed in the tampede.

Renard made his way to the door and hammered on it. A servant ›pened it, and almost as soon as she saw Renard there was a knife in her hand.

"Lady Meredith has been quite clear about what I am to do if you ry to force your way in here," the woman said. "She said to say 'tell lim that last time was about saving the city, but I'm still angry. He's lot welcome.'"

Renard considered pushing his way past the servant, but there was always the chance that she might be serious about the knife. He lesitated a moment too long, and found the door shut in his face, so hat Renard was left for a moment staring up at the façade of the House of Sighs, staring up toward the spot where Meredith's office sat near he top. There was a flicker of movement there that might have been her, or might not.

It was enough to spur Renard on to something stupid. Well, it and he ale he'd had. Renard looked at the wall, trying to pick out a way up at the way he might a rock face. Ordinarily, Renard suspected that it might be impossible to scale; for all its pennants and decorations, there were enough clear spaces on the wall of the House of Sighs to make it smooth and treacherous. They knew about that kind of thing here.

The dragon attack had left its scars on the walls, though, and those provided handholds where otherwise there might not have been any. Renard set his foot in the first spot that might hold him, and started to clamber upwards.

He moved from hold to hold, traversing the face of the House with all the care he might have reserved for a building he was planning to rob. There was nothing secretive about what Renard was doing, though. Not this time.

Below him, he heard cheering, and Renard dared a look down. People were standing there, looking up at him, applauding the audacity of what he was doing. Renard should have basked in that applause. Instead, he ignored them and kept climbing.

His foot slipped, and for a moment, he hung by his hands, so high above the ground below that Renard felt sure that he might shatter if he fell. He *didn't* fall, though, just hung there until his flailing hand managed to catch hold of one of the pennants that hung from the side of the building.

Using it like a rope, Renard continued to climb.

There was a balcony outside Meredith's office. Renard clambered over toward it, putting his foot on a statue, his hand into the crack between two broken bricks. He got a hand on the rail around the balcony's edge.

Meredith stepped out onto her balcony, looking down at him with a mixture of disbelief, confusion, anger, and slight amusement.

"Renard, what are you *doing*?" she demanded, staring down at him.

"Have I told you that you look especially beautiful from this angle?" Renard said.

"And *you* look like a fool," Meredith said. "What are you doing dangling there?"

"I came to see you," Renard said. "I *had* to see you. I wanted to tell you that I love you!"

"You're drunk," Meredith said.

"I'm not drunk," Renard said, and then decided that this was probably a moment for truth. "I'm not *very* drunk. And I'm sober enough to know that I need you. Why won't you let me see you? The last time I was here..."

"The last time you were here, you tried to reconcile with me, and then just days later you were in bed with half of my employees," Meredith snapped back. "You're a drunk, a philanderer, a thief..."

"I have my bad points too," Renard joked, and then caught the look in Meredith's eye. "Meredith, I love you. I feel empty without you. And yes, I... I'm probably all the things you said, but that doesn't mean I love you any less. *Please* give me another chance."

Meredith didn't answer for several seconds. Renard hung there over the city, dangling from the edge of the balcony.

"You could give me a hand up," Renard pointed out.

"I could also push you from the edge and let you drop," Meredith countered. "Aren't you going to promise me fidelity for all time? Undying sobriety? Honesty?"

"Would you believe me if I did?" Renard asked.

He heard Meredith sigh, and she reached down, her hand clamping onto his arm. She was surprisingly strong as she helped him up over the balcony. Renard more or less fell into her arms.

163

"I can promise you that I'll always love you," Renard said. "It was always you, Meredith. It *will* always be you."

He kissed her then, aiming for something heroic, something spectacular. Meredith gave him a coy smile as he pulled back.

"Not bad."

"Not *bad*?" Renard said. "That's it? I climbed a *building* for you."

"You climbed a building because you're the kind of idiot who climbs buildings to make a point," Meredith said. She sighed. "It's just one of the things I love about you. All right, you can stay. But the next time you screw up, I *am* throwing you off the building."

EPILOGUE

Lenore stood behind a set of doors leading to one of the castle's courtyards, feeling as nervous as she ever had in her life. She wore a dress of simple white cloth, the sword Devin had made for her by her side, her crown glittering above it all. It was a little twisted from the violence of the throne room, but it still fit her, and Lenore hadn't had it repaired. It was better that people should remember what they'd all been through to get this far.

"Are you ready?" Orianne asked from her side.

Lenore nodded. "Completely."

At a gesture, the guards on the door opened it, and cheers sounded as Lenore stepped out into the space beyond. By now, Lenore had been through enough wedding preparations in her life, so they opted for the simplest of ceremonies, set in the castle's courtyard so that those who wanted to watch could do so from around them.

There were fewer people allowed to be a part of the ceremony proper, because Lenore didn't want this to be a big thing about which nobles were wearing what, and the order of precedence, and the rest of it. Some were still there, but only the ones who had been in the city, only the ones who had been there for defense of it or the rebuilding.

There were so few people left there. For the first wedding preparations Lenore had been a part of, there had been all her siblings present, and her parents. Now, none of them were left in the kingdom, and the people there were friends, there by choice. Aurelle was wearing a dress of red and grey so dark it was almost mourning black. Lady Meredith stood there with one hand on her shoulder and another keeping a firm grip on the hero Renard's arm, as if he might wander off without that restraint. A small number of Lenore's nobles and the leaders of the Houses, stood around them, and a priest was waiting in their midst.

That was it; so few left after the violence that had marred the kingdom for so long. It was impossible not to think of the fallen with every step, lost to the invasion, to the cruel battles for succession, or to

165

the dragon. There had been her father, cut down by Vars's blade on the eve of the invasion; her mother, executed while Lenore watched.

Lenore felt tears start to fall as she walked, but she kept remembering. The empty spaces where people should have been mattered today, of all days. There had been Rodry, cut down in the act of saving her, and Greave, killed trying to save Nerra from what she had become. Nerra herself had fallen in the battle, and it was only the smallest of consolations to know that she had been fighting to save the city when she died.

Then there was Vars, who now lay in a tomb in one of the family's burial plots. It was unmarked to prevent the violence of all those with reasons to hate him, but Lenore found that she couldn't hate her brother, not now. He'd been a coward, and he'd been cruel because of that cowardice. He'd done unforgivable things. Yet he'd also sacrificed himself at the last in order to save her. That didn't buy Vars absolution, but it meant that Lenore could feel the pain of his passing along with the others.

Plenty who weren't family had died too, and Lenore grieved their loss along with the rest. Odd had been loyal and brave, a man who had given everything in the protection of the realm. Master Grey had been strange and impossible, but had also dedicated his life to keeping the world safe from the threat of returning dragons.

Then there had been the Knights of the Spur, the soldiers who had died in the battles for Royalsport, the ordinary people of the city. Lenore wept for them all, so that by the time she reached the spot where the priest stood, the tears obscured almost everything.

At least, they did until Devin wiped them away. Today, he looked more handsome than he ever had, dressed in simple but well-made clothes, with a cloak of white and gold over the top in an echo of the robes Master Grey used to wear. He had *Loss* by his side, and a staff that he was starting to carve with runes in one hand. They'd agreed to wear the weapons as a reminder of the battles they'd been through to get this far.

"Thinking about everyone we've lost?" Devin asked.

"You read my mind," Lenore managed with a wan smile. "You must be some kind of sorcerer."

"The finest in the land, they tell me," Devin joked. "Or trying to be."

"You'll get there," Lenore said.

166

"And *you* look so beautiful that you must be some kind of princess."

"Not a princess," Lenore corrected him gently. "A queen."

Those were two very different things, because one came with many more obligations than the other.

"You are going to be a great queen," Devin promised her. "And I should know, I'm a magus, remember."

"Of course," Lenore said. Her tears had passed now enough that she could nod to the priest to begin.

He stood there in simple dark robes and spread his hands to take in all those watching.

"My friends, we stand today beneath the sight of the gods to join this man and this woman in matrimony, as they are already joined in love." The priest paused for a moment. "There has been so much destruction in the last months, but this is a moment to create something new. Will any gainsay it?"

No one stepped forward to object to it. Lenore had not expected that anyone would, but even so, it was a relief.

The priest turned to her. Ordinarily, he would have asked the man for his vows first, but Lenore was queen, and that counted for a lot.

"Lenore, Queen of the Northern Kingdom, will you take this man to be your husband? Will you love him for the rest of your days? Will you honor him in your heart, and keep him by your side?"

"I will," Lenore said.

"And you, Devin, Magus of this kingdom, will you take this woman to be your wife? Will you love her for the rest of your days? Will you honor her in your heart, and keep her by your side?"

"I will," Devin promised.

The priest took their hands, laying one atop the other, and bound them together with a length of cloth.

"Then I proclaim you husband and wife. Let none stand between you all your days."

They kissed, and the cheer that followed was enough to nearly deafen Lenore. Bells rang out around the city, and somewhere above, a single dragon passed overhead, its scales shining blue, and a plume of flame bursting out in acknowledgment of the moment.

If it had all been some bard's song, things might have ended there. If it had been one of the stories from Lenore's childhood, things would have been happy forevermore. Lenore wasn't a princess anymore,

167

though, she was a queen, and part of being a queen was that things never quite stopped so neatly. There were still things to do.

"My friends," she called out. "The great hall still needs many repairs, but we can feast here out in the open. Please join us in celebrations, and let a day of feasting be declared in the city. Let food be distributed for that feast."

That raised another cheer, not least because the city was still getting back on its feet after all the violence. There were those in the city who would need that food. Lenore moved over to the others who stood there.

"It is also traditional for a ruler to give out honors on days such as this," Lenore called out to all those watching. "And there are those here who deserve them and more."

She moved to stand before Aurelle first.

"Aurelle, you were my brother's truest love, but more than that, you were the one who carried his cure back to us. Because of you, the House of Scholars will have the means to save those with the scale sickness. You also saved me from traitors to the throne who would have slain me or seen me trapped in a loveless marriage. I name you Lady Aurelle, and raise you to the rank of duchess."

Aurelle dropped into a curtsey, but Lenore helped her up.

"You don't need to do that with me," Lenore said. "Not anymore. You will have the lands and goods that would have gone to Greave. I think he would have wanted that."

"My queen, it's too much."

"It's exactly enough," Lenore assured her.

She moved to stand in front of Renard. Instantly, he looked almost panicked.

"Don't worry, hero of Royalsport," Lenore said. "I'm not going to ennoble you. I *am* going to pardon you, though, for all your crimes before this. It would be embarrassing if my guards had to arrest you now."

"Thank you, my queen."

"Lady Meredith," Lenore said. "There is nothing I can give you without upsetting the balance of the Houses in the city."

"I have everything I want," Meredith assured her. "A ruler who actually cares about the people, for one thing."

"I'm sure the House of Sighs will remind me if I forget," Lenore said.

168

"Oh, it will."

Lenore turned back to Devin, wanting to let the celebrations commence. Only there was a woman coming forward with what looked like a letter in her hands.

"My queen, forgive me," she said. "My name is Sarel. I have carried this message from the Southern Kingdom, from your sister."

Fear rose in Lenore then. Was Erin in danger? Why wasn't she here? Lenore took the letter, opened it, and read swiftly. She found her smile widening as she read.

"Erin has met a man who wants to unite the entire Southern Kingdom, and instead of killing him, she's going to help him?" Lenore said.

"Yes, my queen. It's... complicated."

"And she wants... a peace treaty, trade? Are you *sure* this is from Erin?"

"Yes, my queen," the woman insisted.

"Is everything all right?" Devin asked.

Lenore nodded. "Tell everyone that the celebrations can begin. I'll be there shortly. I have a letter to write to my sister. Would you like to come with me?"

"You need the advice of your royal magus?" Devin asked with a faint smile.

Lenore kissed him. "That wasn't what I had in mind. But yes, always."

They set off together in the direction of the inner keep. Soon, there would be a letter to write, and the complexities of ruling a kingdom damaged by war. Things never really stopped, and maybe that was a good thing. Lenore would need to work out where to start with her sister, and the Southern Kingdom, and all of it. Today might have been a kind of ending, but it was also a beginning.

And maybe that was a good thing.

169

A NEW SERIES—NOW AVAILABLE!

SHADOWSEER: LONDON
(Shadowseer, Book One)

"This novel succeeds—right from the start.... A superior fantasy...It begins, as it should, with one protagonist's struggles and moves neatly into a wider circle...."
–*Midwest Book Review* (re *Rise of the Dragons*)

"Filled with non-stop action, this novel is sure to keep you on the edge of your seat from cover to cover....Rice is setting up for an amazing series to rival series such as Tamora Pierce's Song of the Lioness, with her strong female protagonist making waves in her world and building the confidence of young women in ours."
–*The Wanderer*, A Literary Journal (re *Rise of the Dragons*)

From #1 bestselling author Morgan Rice, a USA Today bestseller and critically-acclaimed author of the fantasy series *The Sorcerer's Ring* (over 3,000 five-star reviews) and the teen fantasy series *The Vampire Journals* (over 1,500 five-star reviews) comes a groundbreaking new series and genre, where fantasy meets mystery.

SHADOWSEER: LONDON (Book One) tells the story of Kaia, 17, an orphan coming of age in the Victorian London of the 1850s. Kaia yearns to escape her horrific orphanage, to discover who her parents were, and to understand why she can sense shadows when others cannot. Yet the streets of London are as brutal as the orphanage, and for Kaia, there is no easy way out.

When Kaia, arrested, faces an even worse punishment, Detective Pinsley, 45, notices a strange marking on her arm and thinks she might be the key in solving a peculiar, mysterious case. Bodies are turning up dead in London, and Pinsley wonders whether it's the work of a deranged serial killer, or of something....else. The methods of murder seem impossible, as does the murderer's ability to escape death.

Kaia is given a choice: help solve the case, or be shipped off to Bedlam, the notorious insane asylum.

Unlikely partners, each mistrusting the other, Kaia and Pinsley embark to scour the dark corners and cobblestone streets of 19th century London in search of clues.

Yet what they find may shock and horrify even them.

Dark fantasy meets mystery in SHADOWSEER, a page-turning, atmospheric thriller packed with authentic period detail, with twists and cliffhangers that will leave you on the edge of your seat. Kaia, a broken hero, will capture your heart as she struggles to claw her way up from the depths, and to solve unsolvable crimes. Fans of books such as *Spellbreaker, The Dresden Files, Mortal Instruments* and *Dr. Jekyl and Mr. Hyde* will find much to love in SHADOWSEER, satisfying fantasy fans who appreciate mystery and suspense, and mystery lovers who want something new, a clean hybrid that will appeal to both adult and young adult readers. Get ready to be transported to another world—and to fall in love with characters you will never forget.

"Morgan Rice proves herself again to be an extremely talented storyteller….This would appeal to a wide range of audiences, including younger fans. It ended with an unexpected cliffhanger that leaves you shocked."
–*The Romance Reviews* (re the paranormal series *Loved*)

"The beginnings of something remarkable are there."
–*San Francisco Book Review* (re the young adult fantasy *A Quest of Heroes*)

SHADOWSEER: PARIS (Book #2), SHADOWSEER: MUNICH (Book #3), SHADOWSEER: ROME (Book #4) and SHADOWSEER: ATHENS (Book #5) are also available.

BOOKS BY MORGAN RICE

SHADOWSEER
SHADOWDEER: LONDON (Book #1)
SHADOWSEER: PARIS (Book #2)
SHADOWSEER: MUNICH (Book #3)
SHADOWSEER: ROME (Book #4)
SHADOWSEER: ATHENS (Book #5)

AGE OF THE SORCERERS
REALM OF DRAGONS (Book #1)
THRONE OF DRAGONS (Book #2)
BORN OF DRAGONS (Book #3)
RING OF DRAGONS (Book #4)
CROWN OF DRAGONS (Book #5)
DUSK OF DRAGONS (Book #6)
SHIELD OF DRAGONS (Book #7)
DREAM OF DRAGONS (Book #8)

OLIVER BLUE AND THE SCHOOL FOR SEERS
THE MAGIC FACTORY (Book #1)
THE ORB OF KANDRA (Book #2)
THE OBSIDIANS (Book #3)
THE SCEPTOR OF FIRE (Book #4)

THE INVASION CHRONICLES
TRANSMISSION (Book #1)
ARRIVAL (Book #2)
ASCENT (Book #3)
RETURN (Book #4)

THE WAY OF STEEL
ONLY THE WORTHY (Book #1)
ONLY THE VALIANT (Book #2)
ONLY THE DESTINED (Book #3)
ONLY THE BOLD (Book #4)

A THRONE FOR SISTERS
A THRONE FOR SISTERS (Book #1)

A COURT FOR THIEVES (Book #2)
A SONG FOR ORPHANS (Book #3)
A DIRGE FOR PRINCES (Book #4)
A JEWEL FOR ROYALS (BOOK #5)
A KISS FOR QUEENS (BOOK #6)
A CROWN FOR ASSASSINS (Book #7)
A CLASP FOR HEIRS (Book #8)

OF CROWNS AND GLORY
SLAVE, WARRIOR, QUEEN (Book #1)
ROGUE, PRISONER, PRINCESS (Book #2)
KNIGHT, HEIR, PRINCE (Book #3)
REBEL, PAWN, KING (Book #4)
SOLDIER, BROTHER, SORCERER (Book #5)
HERO, TRAITOR, DAUGHTER (Book #6)
RULER, RIVAL, EXILE (Book #7)
VICTOR, VANQUISHED, SON (Book #8)

KINGS AND SORCERERS
RISE OF THE DRAGONS (Book #1)
RISE OF THE VALIANT (Book #2)
THE WEIGHT OF HONOR (Book #3)
A FORGE OF VALOR (Book #4)
A REALM OF SHADOWS (Book #5)
NIGHT OF THE BOLD (Book #6)

THE SORCERER'S RING
A QUEST OF HEROES (Book #1)
A MARCH OF KINGS (Book #2)
A FATE OF DRAGONS (Book #3)
A CRY OF HONOR (Book #4)
A VOW OF GLORY (Book #5)
A CHARGE OF VALOR (Book #6)
A RITE OF SWORDS (Book #7)
A GRANT OF ARMS (Book #8)
A SKY OF SPELLS (Book #9)
A SEA OF SHIELDS (Book #10)
A REIGN OF STEEL (Book #11)
A LAND OF FIRE (Book #12)

About Morgan Rice

Morgan Rice is the #1 bestselling and USA Today bestselling author of the epic fantasy series THE SORCERER'S RING, comprising seventeen books; of the #1 bestselling series THE VAMPIRE JOURNALS, comprising twelve books; of the #1 bestselling series THE SURVIVAL TRILOGY, a post-apocalyptic thriller comprising three books; of the epic fantasy series KINGS AND SORCERERS, comprising six books; of the epic fantasy series OF CROWNS AND GLORY, comprising eight books; of the epic fantasy series A THRONE FOR SISTERS, comprising eight books; of the new science fiction series THE INVASION CHRONICLES, comprising four books; of the fantasy series OLIVER BLUE AND THE SCHOOL FOR SEERS, comprising four books; of the fantasy series THE WAY OF STEEL, comprising four books; of the fantasy series AGE OF THE SORCERERS, comprising eight books; and if the new fantasy series SHADOWSEER, comprising three books (and counting). Morgan's books are available in audio and print editions, and translations are available in over 25 languages.

Morgan loves to hear from you, so please feel free to visit www.morganricebooks.com to join the email list, receive a free book, receive free giveaways, download the free app, get the latest exclusive news, connect on Facebook and Twitter, and stay in touch!

Made in the USA
Las Vegas, NV
02 December 2022